THE HOUSE of ONTARIO

ROYCE MacGILLIVRAY

Edited by Vivian Webb

Illustrated by Mark Grice

The House of Ontario
written by Royce MacGillivray
published by
Natural Heritage/Natural History Inc.
P.O. Box 69, Postal Station H
Toronto, Ontario
N4C 5H7

Design and Production   Derek Chung Tiam Fook
Illustrated by Mark Grice

Typesetting   Compositor Associates Limited

Copyright © 1983

First Printing, July 1983

Canadian Cataloguing in Publication Data

MacGillivray, Royce.
    The House of Ontario

ISBN 0-920474-31-4

1. Ontario — History, Comic, satirical, etc.
I. Title.

FC3061.3.M32   971.3'002'07   C83-098294-9
F1057.6.M32

CONTENTS

Published by Natural Heritage/Natural History Inc. with a grant in-aid-of publication from the Ontario Heritage Foundation, Ministry of Citizenship and Culture.

TO THE READER

It has long been evident to me that much of the best (in the sense of the liveliest and the most informative) history of Ontario appears in the books and articles of local historians. The following pages are my attempt to write a mythical history of Ontario in a series of fictitious extracts from the works of a number of supposed or imaginary writers, most of whom are local historians. I hope many of these extracts will be found amusing, but I also hope that the reader will sometimes find, in the midst of reading fiction, that he is glimpsing with renewed vividness a world which existed only yesterday. This world shaped the lives of many of us and still has the power to make us feel, when we meet it in imagination and memory, that we have come home again.

Royce MacGillivray

This page intentionally left blank

FIRST SETTLERS

A GOOD BUSINESS

A GOOD BUSINESS

Our ancestor received his farm as a United Empire Loyalist. I am sorry to say he was shabbily treated by the authorities. They allotted him a poorer farm than his neighbours. In the spring the water lay on his farm till June. He had bad neighbours. Not one of them would help him with the ditching. A kind of bramble known to the pioneers as the Poison Rose grew profusely on his property. He tried to cut it down but the more he cut, the more it sprang up again. His wife was sickly all this time. She was so weak she could not work in the fields. Her brothers were ungrateful. All of them told lies about him. You can see his life was hard. About this time he saw that circumstances were against him. He tried to sell his farm to a missionary but the missionary would not buy it.

Then the thought came to him, "Why not open a mill?" So he dammed up the stream on his property. Afterwards he built the mill. There were no stones on his property, so he had to pay a man to haul them from a mile away to make the foundations. He got the money from his parents. The mill did badly. This was because the Justices of the Peace were against him and cautioned the people against using his mill. Still, he managed to make a living. It was not very good, but it was enough. He was a man of simple tastes. People had to be in those days.

His wife died on 29 November 1796. A tree fell on her. She was buried in the family cemetery behind the house. Unfortunately this cemetery was not fenced in. People knew at the time where it was, but soon its location was forgotten. By this wife he had six children. He married again to give the children a mother. His new wife was a very good woman. Unfortunately her relatives were not. They gave him a hard time. He had to borrow money from them to pay for ditching his farm. He had many a story to tell about how hard they were in demanding repayment. Once, when he went into the blacksmith's shop, his father-in-law said, "Here comes the beggar." That is what he had to put up with.

His wife was always after him to leave the farm. She wanted them to live in York but he disagreed. He said it was too small. He said the United States was the place of opportunity. If they went some place, they should go there. He had many fond memories of the United States from his youth. But this proved not to be necessary. His luck changed. One day one of the Justices of the Peace who had been so against him came to see him. This man was very apologetic. It took him a long time to come to the point and state his business. You could see he was ashamed of the way he had treated a good man. It is always best to have a clear conscience. At last he came to the point. There was a job to be done in Cornwall. Would our ancestor do it? He would. Soon other jobs opened up for him all over the province.

He travelled a great deal. The demand for him was not heavy, but it was steady. He was so good at his job that no one ever tried to take it away from him. This was at a time when jobs were scarce. The farm was run by his eldest son and prospered. So everything was going very well. His son even found a way to cut down the brambles. All the younger children went to school in Boston. His wife's family was jealous and cast him off completely. He did not mind. He made the joke that he would meet one or two of them again in his line of business. This joke was often repeated. All the pioneers loved a good joke to relieve the tedium of their labours.

He lived to a ripe old age. He was much against William Lyon Mackenzie and his rebels. He was retired when Mackenzie and his rebels made their attempt against the Queen and failed. He was accustomed to say, while the trials were proceeding, that his fingers itched to be back at his old trade again. He died on his old farm on New Year's Day 1840. His son was a Tartar for work but even he apparently did not believe in keeping up cemeteries. Therefore we do not know our ancestor's exact resting place. We should all be grateful to be descended from this stout pioneer.

MRS. F. HASPWELL, *A Genealogy (1952).*

THE LUMMECKS

It is still to be hoped, even at this late date, that a specimen of the principal Ontario cactus, the Lummecks, so cherished by the pioneers, will some day be found in some isolated hardwood grove. One of the wet-soil cactuses, its stout, pale-green stems rose to a height of six feet above the forest mould. Powerful, foot-long spines protected its succulent flesh against all but the most hunger-maddened animal predators. But these terrifying spines were no match for the pioneer axe, and the pink flesh of the cactus, tasting, it is said, much like muskmelon, was more common even than maple syrup on every pioneer table. Indeed it was the old timers' view that syrup-making was never much pursued by the pioneers till driven to it by the near extinction of the Lummecks. The last known stand of Lummecks was found lurking in a grove around an abandoned house a few miles north of Waterloo in 1919. Unfortunately it was destroyed by a raiding party of specialty-food entrepreneurs from Buffalo before a research team from the University of Chicago could reach it.

P. HORZEN, *The Woods Our Fathers Knew (1969).*

ANCIENT TECHNOLOGIES

Fifty years ago the land on which this prosperous village stands was an unbroken forest, trodden only by the unleathered foot of the red man. When Jonathan Olem arrived to set up his shanty beside the Rapids, he was a young man of 25, newly arrived from the Thirteen Colonies. Today the patriarch of our village, whose snow-white beard reminds us of the many winters he has seen, he loves nothing better than to recall the means used by himself and the other heroes of his day to fell the giants of the forests.

For those of us who imagine that the good axe, and only the good axe, was the tool used by the pioneers for this task, he has only a twinkle in his eyes as he reflects how little this later, softer generation understands of the methods of their forefathers. How, he asks, can you cut a tree trunk 12 feet across with an axe? In the face of the question we are dumb. But he tells us the answer.

The giant tree could be gradually hollowed out by fire, creating a "cave" over which it would gradually collapse. Or, in a technique which the Indians taught the settlers, it could be undermined by tunnels and its multitudinous roots severed one by one till the tree, having lost its foundation, was caught by the wind and toppled. The knowledge of botany that this pursuit of the roots through tunnels required needs not to be emphasized.

Following another Indian method, a deadly acid was brewed by the pioneer housewives in their clay kettles from a common berry that grew in the forest then. A line of acid would be painted around the tree trunk on the first dry day in the spring, followed by other applications on successive days, till the tree was burnt through to the centre. By skilful calculation of the curves to be followed by the line of acid, it was possible to determine with the utmost precision the direction in which the tree would fall. A mathematician from Oxford University who observed the curves is said to have written them down in a book using the little marks and signs that the men who study mathematics use when they want to describe something very exactly.

But why, we ask our patriarch, have these amazing techniques of the early men of the forest been abandoned? Why is the backwoodsman of today, as he rolls back the forest, wholly reliant on the axe and saw? And we gather from a few well-chosen words from our pioneer that a reliance on an iron technology, to which he and his fellow settlers could never be party, has eroded the ingenuity and resourcefulness of an earlier and better day.

J. HOOPS, *Elms and Olems (1835).*

HORNTON

Many pioneer communities harbour memories of the gruelling adventures on ship which preceded their landing in the New World, but no community, perhaps, has a stranger tale to tell in this respect than Hornton. The ship, *Palm Grove*, Captain J. Leeds, from Liverpool, was driven far south by gales in the spring of 1802 and there, to the terror of its passengers, it was attacked and mastered by a pirate ship from the Barbary Coast of Africa.

Captain Leeds and those of his crew who survived the attack were hurled alive into the shark-infested waters while the terrified passengers watched helplessly. The captain of the pirates was an Englishman who had been living in Barbary since his parents were captured by pirates when he was a baby. He compelled the terrified immigrants to accept him and his crew among their numbers and all sailed together in two ships — the *Palm Grove* and the pirate vessel — to Quebec City. From there they made their way to Upper Canada where land had been reserved for the immigrants. Bona fide immigrants and pirates alike settled down to the task of clearing the forest and making a life for themselves in the New World. In the comradeship and shared tasks of a pioneer community the distinction between pirates and captives was soon obliterated. All dwelt in peace and friendship together and early and frequent intermarriage has ensured that there are none among the older families of Hornton who cannot claim descent from both groups.

P. ZOG, *Hornton (1965)*.

Of the unanswered questions in the religious history of this province, none is more intriguing than how an element of Mohammedanism became established among the earliest settlers of Hornton. One tradition asserts that the native butler of a retired general from British India preached it among the people in rivalry with the Christian missionaries who had just begun to circulate in this newly-settled part of the province. A mosque was maintained in Hornton by the older settlers as late as the 1830s, when William Lyon Mackenzie visited it and denounced Bishop Macdonell and Archdeacon Strachan for sowing Mohammedanism in the province. When some of the settlers, worn out by old age and incessant labour, retired to Toronto in the 1840s to enjoy their last years in the ease to which their hard-earned savings had entitled them, they seem to have been the mainstays of the semi-secret mosque on Bloor Street which is sometimes mentioned in memoirs of the time. After that we have no evidence of any religion except Presbyterianism among the Hornton settlers or their descendants.

12

The surviving influence of Mohammedanism, however, may help explain why L'Easten Township, to which Hornton belongs, was one of the leading temperance areas in the province as late as the 1950s. In temperance publications it was often called simply the *"Banner Township"*, implying that in the temperance cause it *"led the parade"*.

R. DIT, *Pioneer Religion (1950).*

IT HAPPENS ALL THE TIME

AMAZING FACTS FROM THE HISTORY OF URLAR COUNTY

In 1829 a syndicate bought the entire town of Urlar, after the iron mine failed, with the intention of burning it to make potash. The furniture in the houses, as well as the houses, and even the frame church together with the wooden headstones and coffins in the cemetery were burnt for this purpose. When the town was three-quarters gone what remained was purchased by the Canada Company as a rest home for its employees . . . After a quarrel with his wife, Osbert Wilkson, of County Centre, spent four years sulking in a dry well till driven out by the rainy years 1842 and 1843 . . . Lawyer Seth Wood of Urlar Station had five wives, outlived them all, and broke the last will and testament of every one of them . . . Tena Aranagusim and her family never knew for sure what country they came from. When the bailiff and his guard dogs had shepherded the people of the village down to the wharf while their huts were burning behind them he spoke softly to them. He assured the villagers that they were going with the love of their landlord, who was a good man and only anxious that they should acquire in Canada the freedom and affluence they could never hope for in the Old World. And much more of the same. When the departing boat with its wailing passengers was only a dozen yards from the shore, the bailiff called from the wharf in his loudest voice, *"Remember, if you want to come back, this place is called SCOTLAND."* Afterwards, the emigrants began to have their doubts.

J. RAIKES, *Urlar County (1887).*

MYTH

If we enquire for the evidence of the existence of the swarms of passenger pigeons that are alleged to have thronged this province, we draw a complete blank. The members of our research commune, financed by a two-year grant, have combed the relevant literature — census returns, assessment rolls, merchants' papers, lawyers' papers, farm records, wills, diaries, autobiographies and histories — without being able to find a single trace of the numerous merchants or entrepreneurs who were supposed to have flourished shipping barrels of salted pigeons down the St. Lawrence to Montreal. Nor have they found a single trace of anyone who ever paid a storekeeper's debt in passenger pigeons or killed pigeons to raise money to discharge his mortgage or indeed any trace of anyone who ever saw a passenger pigeon at all. It is evident that an enormous hoax has been perpetrated, but in whose interest? The question is not hard to answer. Nascent capitalism always needs scapegoats to answer for its own inadequacies. In this case a myth was deliberately created to the effect that starvation and alienation were not created by the cruel incapacities of capitalism, but were caused by the failure of enormous (though as we have seen, imaginary) flocks of pigeons which once allegedly darkened the sky, bringing free food to the people.

KUXDORF AND FLOOMP, eds. *Studies, (1972).*

TRAIL OF THE FRENZ

One of the earliest examples of severe punishment of a civilian in the province was that of a man called Frenz, who was sentenced to receive 200 lashes. My father was a soldier in the British Army at the time and was called upon to do bugler's duty in connection with carrying out the sentence. Frenz was marched out to the garrison parade ground manacled and under heavy guard. He had been convicted of selling to the fur traders some rations set aside for the sustenance of Loyalist orphans. He had just made some reply to the effect that he was a relative of persons of eminence in England when the first blow of the cat took his breath away. A half hour later he was dragged from the parade ground pouring blood and all but lifeless. I heard later that he benefited so little from his experience that on his recovery he stole a large sum of money from the Adjutant-General and headed for Indian country with his fur trader friends and two or three of the orphans, whom, incredibly, he had enticed into his employ.

COLONEL BUCKMINSTER, *The Goodness of the Good Old Days (1867).*

It is much to be feared that many remarkable forms of plant and animal life vanished in the ruthless process of clearing the land of this new province. When my great-grandfather Frenz came to this township, its cedar swamps had been recently swept away by forest fires set by squatters. And in the ashy waste that was left, the settlers found the skeletons of several enormous snakes, one more than 80 feet long and with a rib cage nearly two feet in width. Charred meat still clinging to the bones of these giants showed that their deaths had been as recent as the fires. For years the pioneers of this area went in terror of meeting one of these snakes alive, but as that never happened we must conclude that happily for the poor pioneers, but unhappily for science, these snakes had become an extinct species.

P. FRENZ, *To My Children (1888).*

Though often wonderfully shrewd in their own line of business, many of the old pioneer merchants were veritable children in affairs outside their daily path. My father knew an old gentleman who grew rich on a good trade with the settlers, not to speak of a profitable grist and carding mill he ran along with a nice sideline in mortgages. But this same gentleman was so gullible that a notorious charlatan called Frenz sold him several barrels full of bones, alleging them to be the ribs of a giant snake found in the ashes of a burnt-out swamp. Frenz had acquired these by some legal chicanery from the estate of the old provincial surveyor, Cutlass and it was later learned that he had successfully peddled these barrels at points as far away as Vermont and northern Pennsylvania.

T. ROODS, *Byways and Bygones (1879).*

TRAVELLERS

When my great-great-grandfather and his brother settled on their lot in Russell County in 1802, they found in the dense forest that covered their land a collection of weathered log houses clustered close together. Some of them were little more than huts but others were of considerable size and elegance. One was graced by a log tower which in its tottering state rose above the height of the hard maples. All the roofs had collapsed and trees grew riotously through what had once been the floors and ceilings of the houses. My great-great-grandfather and his brother could find no clue as to who had built these houses. Log houses are a particularly durable form of building and it appeared from all other circumstances that they could not indeed be of very recent date.

I am afraid that all that remained of these log structures was reduced to ashes in the next few years for the manufacture of potash. Even the field stones that made up the foundations were removed to clear the land for plowing and are today indistinguishable from the other stones in the fences that line the fields.

Having more leisure than my pioneer ancestors, and having more sentimentality toward the past than they had, I longed for years to know who built this mysterious hamlet deep in the Canadian forest years before any white settlers are known to have been in these parts.

I am as far from answering this question now as when I began but meantime I have accumulated a quantity of information that can hardly fail to be of interest to archaeologists. Almost by accident I encountered in a North Carolina newspaper a report of a similar hamlet having been found in the North Carolina forest by a settler in the 1600s. Many enquiries and much research in archives turned up three similar references, dating from 1620 to 1867. But most surprising, when the locations of the five hamlets of which I now had record were plotted on a map, they formed virtually a straight line, from North Carolina to my great-great-grandfather's farm. This line gave me a new clue to follow and by careful study of land and family records and old newspapers from towns along that line, I discovered more than 20 such hamlets. I now had an almost straight line of them stretching from a point a few miles from the sea near Wilmington, N.C., to a point in the old logging country west of Quebec City. Obviously, along this line many of the mysterious hamlets had vanished without being reported, but those for which I had locations were all distant from other hamlets by 23 miles or multiples of 23 miles. The only piece of wood I have been able to procure suitable for radiocarbon dating gives a reading of about 100 years and is obviously spurious. I ought not to have paid an antique dealer $500 for it. I continue to search for genuine samples of wood from which a reliable dating can be made.

Meanwhile I continue to collect data and to speculate on what resolute people, motivated by what goals, landed on the North Carolina seacoast some centuries ago and by slow progress (was each hamlet, as I suspect, a wintering place, marking the end of another summer's journey?) moved in a wonderfully straight line into the wilderness of the Canadian Shield.

I am an old man and no explorer, but I hand on to those younger than I the next task, which is to trace this line as far as it goes into the north. I have come to feel over the years that in some way I have a deep, instinctive understanding of the minds of these wonderful people, whose very colour, clothes and features I nevertheless cannot in the least envisage. I suspect, on the basis of these notions, that the line will end in the northern waters as mysteriously as it began.

P. BEC, *Point-on-a-Line, My Father's Farm (1978)*.

MISHAM WATERS

The fortunes of the Misham family were made by a farseeing act of speculation. When the first surveyors came in the spring of 1798 to this part of the new province, they found an extensive lake covering the whole of what is today Misham County and a bit more. The surveyors prepared to run their lines around the lake, but Colonel Misham, a noted linguist, in conversing with the Indians learned that the lake was so insubstantial and shallow that it normally disappeared by late July. Keeping this information to himself, the Colonel offered to accept the entire piece of ground covered by the lake as a complete settlement of his claims on the Crown if it could be granted quickly to him. The Crown officials hastened to accept an offer so evidently advantageous to the King.

Within a few years the Colonel had the lake bed so effectively drained by several well-placed outlets that it never flooded again. He had the surveyors map out an entire county, complete with townships, concessions, road allowances, Crown and Clergy Reserves, town sites and individual lots within the boundaries of the lake. He named this county, which had so surprisingly risen from the waters, after himself. The remaining lots which fell within the boundaries of the old lake but outside the rectangle of his county he permitted to be incorporated within the boundaries of the adjacent counties, although he retained ownership of them.

If the Mishams of the next two generations had not been so unhappily addicted to opium and litigation — one of them is said in a publication of the 1960s to have been the first drug pusher in the province — it is probable they would have made a mark on the politics of Upper Canada and Canada West. As it is, it is believed that the last of the Mishams, another Colonel, contributed the funds that made possible the rise of Sir John A. Macdonald. On account of the Colonel's earlier financing of the Mackenzie Rebellion, this contribution had long to be kept a secret.

In the 1960s and '70s a housing subdivision flowed over the historic Misham County like the returning waters and the name is expected soon to be changed to the Borough of Misham.

C. CLOSEN, *Misham (1979)*.

BURIED

Where the first settler of Agricolaville located his cabin has long been a matter of controversy. I often questioned my father and other oldtimers on this point. Their evidence, when carefully sifted and compared, points to the following conclusion. There was, at the ford in the river, a broad bank of sand which at most times remained hard and dry but at certain wet seasons turned into a gurgling bed of quicksand. It is supposed that the first settler established his cabin there, and it was in that cabin that the traveller Lord Cotswold interviewed him in 1838. Cotswold describes this first settler in his book of travels as a wild man of the forest, *bearded and morose* and much resembling in every respect a well-known King's Bench Judge of the last generation. Unfortunately he neglects to mention the settler's name.

The year 1840 was a year of high water and it is to be feared that the settler and his cabin were suddenly engulfed in the sands. As late as my grandfather's time farmers occasionally lost cows on this shore by a sudden instability of the sands in a wet season. It was believed that the sharp hoofs of the cattle fatally punctured the surface tension of the sand when it had been undermined from below by the rising waters. This dangerous bank was dredged away when the paper mill was built in 1920. I have been unable to discover what became of certain timbers and an ancient dark lantern said to have been recovered from the sands at this time. The location has been an outlet for mill waste for many years. If it is ever restored to more salubrious uses, it is to be hoped that a marker will be placed there to commemorate the founder of one of Canada's most diversified manufacturing cities.

B. MURCHUSON, *Years of Progress (1981)*.

DISCOVERY IN THE FOREST

In the earliest times the northern half of this county was a dense primeval forest. The descendants of the pioneers often retold stories of the cave-like gloom of the forest floor where the first poor log shanties were built. In those days fires would sometimes run along the thick needle beds of the forest floor and, leaping upwards, engulf miles of towering pines in a conflagration that must have been as terrifying as a nuclear explosion. In

1832 a family from Upper Silesia called Zast came to this sombre, explosive forest to live.

Zasts are common today in the pleasant farmland which has replaced this primeval forest, but the stranger to the county may be surprised to learn that not a single descendant of the first Zast family is among them. In every case the Zast name is an adopted one. To explain how this came about we must penetrate an historical darkness almost as formidable as the gloomy forests the first Zasts inhabited.

It appears that one morning when the Zasts were breaking up a little ground for a potato garden they came upon the hub of a wheel poking out of the earth. And investigating a little more, they uncovered the whole of a wheeled wagon, carefully disassembled and buried at a shallow depth. Sleeping among the portions of their vehicle were the skeletons of a man and a woman and a child. A few coins in the scraps of a purse indicated from their dates that they had been buried there about the time of the coming of the Loyalists. The Zasts called their few, widely-scattered neighbours to view what they had uncovered. One of the oldest residents recalled a story, once current among the Indians of the district, that an American tribe of Indians had murdered a party of settlers in the pine forest. It appeared they had superstitiously assumed that the wheeled vehicle was in some way a living being and "killed it" by dismembering it. They sought to placate its soul by giving it a respectable burial among its owners.

The skeleton of the man, woman and child were reburied in the pioneer cemetery and the non-metal parts of their vehicle were burned. It appeared to the Zasts that the bones of the horses must also have been buried nearby but when a cursory search revealed nothing, it was assumed that perhaps the Indians had seen their way clear to seize the beasts for their own uses. In a busy pioneer community the whole incident quickly faded into the back of people's minds. The Zasts themselves, however, through the pioneer love of nicknames, came to be known as *the Skeletons*.

In every pioneer community there appear to have been one or two individuals who were pre-Adamites, as it were, having been there as squatters or drifters before the coming of the "first" settlers, who often were only "first" in the sense of being the earliest respectable, hard-working people. The pine forest had one such pre-Adamite, an old man known only as Zeb, who had lived, it was said, among Indians in the States during most of his early life. He now lived alone, in filth and near starvation, in a hut of pine roots he had built against the one surviving wall of an abandoned cabin.

I do not know how it was that my grandfather became acquainted and even intimate with him, but one day he learned something which interested and disturbed him — the history of the dead family of United Empire Loyalists. They were Jordwells from Maine and had come into the forest

DISCOVERY IN THE FOREST

with their wagon pulled not by horses but by six young men, of whom this ancient derelict was one. The nature of the influence which the Jordwells applied to their six human horses my grandfather could never precisely determine, but it was supported by a vigorous and steady application of the whip which left them thoroughly bloodied and a feast for the merciless flies and mosquitoes. The murders had been committed, of course, by the human horses, not by Indians. The murderers had all fled from the scene except for this old man, and he believed (though on what evidence my grandfather could never determine) that they were all dead. The old man, being a murderer, was answerable to the law, but seeing that the crime had been committed over 50 years before, and probably with justification, and that the old man was now little more than an imbecile, my grandfather kept what he had learned to himself, intending to reveal it only when the old man was dead.

Time passed. The two Canadas were united in 1841 into the single Province of Canada and my grandfather was a member of the first legislature of the new British province. Being now acquainted with cities and with a wider society than before, he found opportunity to make enquiries about the Jordwells. An old clerk in the government land office, who remembered the case, led him to the documents. The Jordwells had come to Canada originally as political refugees but their claims for land grants were stopped by objections that they were guilty of a series of murders in a sailors' lodging house they had run in Philadelphia. Somehow they managed to acquire enough political influence to have these objections overruled and were granted a large tract of land on the far side of the pine forest. They also managed to become guardians of six young male orphans and took them along when they left Montreal, promising to settle them within 10 years as independent farmers on a part of their own grant. These, all too evidently, became their luckless steeds. Neither the Jordwells nor their wards were ever heard of by officialdom again and their land was granted to later settlers. Their file contained only a single letter of recent years. That was from a family in Upper Silesia, called Zast, who asked how they could acquire land as near as possible to the place where the Jordwells were last seen. With the knowledge that the Zasts had not made their discovery completely without knowledge of what they were about to uncover, my grandfather prepared to question them on his return to the pine forest.

A member of the legislative assembly, which my grandfather was, was a man of some standing in those days. The Zasts quickly dropped their professions of ignorance and told a story which was to be told and retold in the kitchens of the county for the next generation. Their father had been one of the murderers of the Jordwells. He had afterwards fled to sea and, after service in Napoleon's armies, deserted and settled in Upper Silesia. There he married and among his children were the settlers who eventually came to Canada. The murderer's conscience had never left him at peace. He implored his son to go to Canada and see that his victims were given Christian burial, without which, he said, he could not rest in the grave. When the settler Zast had related these facts to my grandfather, he added that he had done what his father had requested of him, and had settled happily in the New World. But now, seeing that his father's crimes were revealed, nothing remained for him and his family but to pack up and resettle themselves somewhere on the American frontier. My grandfather replied that this would not be necessary, for he could keep a secret as well as any man. But the next morning the Zasts were gone, having reduced their neat log buildings to debris in the night. My grandfather went to the old imbecile who lived in the pine-root hut to see what further information he could glean from him. He found him more inarticulate than ever but with a message from Mr. Zast, which he was ordered to deliver to my grandfather if ever he should call. The message was simple. It said, "Beware a man called McIntee." A couple of weeks later word reached the settlement that the entire Zast family had perished in a gale when crossing Lake Ontario on their way to their new American home. The following winter the old imbecile died. It seemed that all human links with the murder which had so unpromisingly begun the history of our neighbourhood had now been severed.

But my grandfather's inquiries into the records had not, it appeared, gone unreported to higher quarters and the scanty press of the province had begun to print titbits on the story of the murders in the pine forest. A party of lumbermen in the employ of a wealthy Montreal merchant called McIntee appeared and began to strip the trees off certain tracts of land to which McIntee had acquired cutting rights.

My grandfather at once remembered the Zasts' message and in October of one year escaped two assassination attempts on his life staged by the lumbermen. He could not have done so had he not been so opportunely warned and he remained everlastingly grateful to the Zasts. The lumberers departed as mysteriously as they had come. The night they left, ferocious, wind-driven fires sent long fingers of destruction into the farms and villages of the pine forest. It was only by an abrupt dropping of the wind, followed by the beginning of a long, soaking autumn rain the next day, that the settlement was saved. In the years that followed, whenever my grandfather was settling old country settlers on lands in the pine forest, he tried to persuade them to change their name to Zast and that is why there are so many Zasts in our county today.

MRS. ZAST SMITH, *The Pine Forest and the Zasts (1948)*.

EDWARD GIBBON

Our village was founded by a U.E. Loyalist called Captain Carlson Gribbling. His wife, the daughter of an English general, had in her earliest years been an especial favourite of the historian Edward Gibbon, whose partiality for the conversation of attractive young ladies is well known. We may suppose that Mrs. Gribbling's life in Canada was not an easy one. No less than 21 children did the Captain father upon her before she died in childbed. The Captain replaced her with another — the legendary Mrs. Tyler — who is said to have drowned him in his own mill pond as soon as his fifth paralytic fit left him defenceless.

The first Mrs. Gribbling has an honoured place in the history of our village and by rights should have similar place in the history of Canada. It is said that in emulation of Edward Gibbon she originally planned to write a major history of the British in North America. Perhaps for the wife of a wealthy Philadelphian such as she was for a few happy years that would have been possible. But in our village all historical avenues but one were closed to her, and that led her to write the history, laboriously and microscopically detailed, of this tiny village. She filled more than 5,000 folio pages with the history, day by day and sometimes hour by hour, of the village from the morning of her arrival in June 1785, when the Captain first reached the falls in the river, drank a bottle of whisky with his workmen and drove down the stake to mark the site of his mill, to her death 17 years later.

In her lifetime she came only once to press. The Captain, who while a bully and blackguard was not without a taste for the arts, had established a small printing press in his grist mill and operated it with the aid of his waterwheel. On that celebrated press he published the 18 volumes — of priceless value now — of the famous "Loyalist Poets", whose efforts mark the beginning of the literature of Ontario. There too he published, though we can imagine with much grumbling, the single, golden, 150-page volume of his wife's FIRST DAY IN THE HISTORY OF GRIBBLING, U.C. It is no exaggeration to say that this simple volume, as well-written as a novel and as fact-filled as an encyclopedia, is worth more as a historical source on the foundation of the province than all the histories to be published in the next 50 years. Once, and for a single day, we see the Loyalists as they really were. It has been truly said of this volume that to have read it is to have lived in the village from the dawn to dusk of that single day.

It follows that the remainder of Mrs. Gribbling's manuscript would be of inestimable value if it could be found. As it turned out, about 20 years after the Captain's death a most remarkable burial mound was found in the swamps of an outlying part of the county. An adult Indian, apparently a priest or chief or other person of importance, had been buried in full body armour made of clay similar to that of the broken Indian pottery found in the old campsites along the rivers. Most surprisingly, the clay seems to have been baked onto the body after death. The slowly-spreading reports of this discovery brought a few men of learning hurrying from distant parts of the globe to examine the mound and try to buy its treasures from the settlers — who were perhaps, in the minds of these savants, not much less savage than the Indian who had lain, for no one knew how many centuries, in the earth. The great Alexander von Humboldt sent his cousin and John Quincy Adams, the ex-president of the United States, sent the brilliant Louis Aggasiz. But before these luminaries could arrive the rich prize was secured for $100 and carried off by an anonymous young German scholar who happened to be travelling through northern Ontario in search of hitherto unrecorded Indian obstetrical customs and vowel and consonantal shifts. Being shown Mrs. Gribbling's manuscript as a further curiosity of the neighbourhood, he recognized its value at once and, for an additional $1, added it to his booty. From that day to this Mrs. Gribbling's manuscript has never been seen by any Canadian.

The Indian in ceramic armour disappeared as completely till almost the end of the 19th century, when the execution for treason of a high-ranking Russian nobleman led to the dispersal of his art collection and the purchase of part of it, including the armour-covered Indian, by Czar Nicholas II. Attempts at this time by Goldwin Smith and by Professor James Mavor of the University of Toronto to trace the history of the Indian in the intervening years in hopes that it would lead to the recovery of Mrs. Gribbling's manuscript proved fruitless. Noting their efforts, the *Toronto Globe* lamented, in mock-Gibbonian terms, *"It is to be hoped, and is perhaps probable, that one day the book of the first and perhaps greatest historian of Ontario will come to light and be published and the world will marvel that the HISTORIAN OF THE ROMAN EMPIRE had a perceptive and profound disciple even in the darkness of the Canadian forest."*

Scholars are inclined today to reject a theory, advanced in the 1940s by Professor Deireadh Fomhair of the University of Toronto, that a 20-volume history of villages (*kishlaki*) in the Tadzhik Soviet Socialist Republic published at Dushanbe by the Organized People's Publishing House between 1938 and 1940 was basically a translation of Mrs. Gribbling's work. Similarly, little favour has been shown to the view that the manuscript never went any further than New York and was the sole source for the towering reputation of a voluminous historian of the American frontier. I myself remain optimistic, on the basis of some private correspondence with Russian scholars, that the complete manuscript may yet be returned to Canada for publication.

KATE OSWALD, *Mrs. Gribbling and Her Book (1968).*

A LATE LOYALIST

Lampsden is today so peaceful and prosperous a town, full of citizens so public-spirited and independent minded, that it is difficult to believe that it had its origins in a slave colony. Yet this is the story we learn from the oldest and most accurate records and from the most authentic local traditions.

It appears that about 1796 a *"Late Loyalist"* from Boston, by the name of Colonel Hecklem, settled in this portion of the forest, drew up the plan of a town and, without troubling to have the provincial authorities grant him the land, began placing settlers on it. The settlers, however, were obtained in most unusual ways. The Colonel or his agents (of which one Redstone was especially notorious) would meet the immigrant ships at Quebec and agree with the most poverty-stricken immigrants to provide them with a livelihood in return for accepting indentured servant status for a few years. Once in the Colonel's colony, the hapless settlers found themselves trapped in a system where penalties were assessed for every insignificant breach of the Colonel's rigid code, with each penalty adding a few more years to the term of the immigrant's servitude. A government commission of inquiry in 1825 found that most servants who had been in the Colonel's service for more than five years had increased their period of servitude beyond 100 years. By one of the Colonel's rules, wives and children also worked as indentured servants to reduce their husbands' and fathers' periods of servitude.

The Colonel and Redstone also welcomed into their colony children whose parents had died on the immigrant ships and orphans from the streets of Montreal and Quebec. They bought orphans freely from civic authorities, who welcomed this means of relieving themselves of the burden of their support. They also bought children from indigent parents, who were happy to reduce the brood in their little packed log cabins in return for a few shillings or a bucket of flour. To all these unfortunates, however obtained, the Colonel assigned the status of slave for life, with the further stipulation that their children, if any, would also be slaves.

The result was, for a time at least, a boom town. Lampsden by 1810 had two saw and two grist mills, a woollen factory, an ashery, a newspaper noted for its thoughtful editorials and investigative reporting, called *Redstone's Weekly*, a workshop in which 50 blacksmiths worked to turn out products at prices that swept rival blacksmiths out of business for a distance of a three days journey in every direction and a large agricultural force that laboured on the Colonel's wheat and potato plantations. Other slaves worked in the Colonel's mansion and in the communal cafeterias and dormitories. The conservative traveller Harriet Isman, who visited the colony about this time, thought slavery *"an even more enviable system"* at Lampsden than *"in the best southern plantations"* and argued that the Colonel, if eligible as a Loyalist, should be given a peerage.

The Colonel's relations with the government before the War of 1812 are a mystery. Orders from London repeatedly demanded the closure of his slave colony but were ignored by the provincial authorities. In the provincial legislature the colony was, mysteriously, never once mentioned. The Colonel's connection with the powerful North West Company, which bought much of its farm produce from his estates and made him a partner in 1810, perhaps contributed to his immunity. In the War of 1812, when American natives and late-arriving Loyalists were suspect, the Colonel demonstrated his loyalty by loans to the government and by providing free work forces for building roads and bridges for troop use.

From this period we have our only portrait of the Colonel during his years in Canada. Said to have been painted by the Boston portrait painter Paul Revere Widderstand, it shows an angry-looking man with protruding eyes, a fuzzy swirl of white hair around a glistening bald spot, long curling red moustaches and a bushy, almost circular red beard. In his lap he holds his favourite cats, Washington and Valley Forge.

Despite his services to the government, his regime did not long outlive the war. In 1816 (*"The Year without a Summer"*) and in the next few years famine scourged the province. The Colonel and Redstone were busier than ever before, buying up children from destitute parents and even, sometimes, accepting whole families into the state of slavery. From one log cabin in Lambton County, 14 children, ranging in age from six months to 16 years, together with their parents, six bachelor uncles, four maiden aunts and two cousins with one able-bodied grandfather all followed the Colonel into his slave colony, leaving only a decrepit grandmother and grandfather in their 90s to occupy the deserted hut. This aged couple died within a few weeks from cold and malnutrition, having no food but a few potatoes supplied to them occasionally by some neighbours who lived 20 miles away. At the same time, the Colonel diverted part of his labour force to opening a lead mine in the Laurentians north of Hawkesbury and attempted to begin a new colony a few miles north of Oshawa.

The public outcry could no longer be ignored and in 1819 the provincial government unseated Colonel Hecklem by ordering him to leave the Crown land he was illegally occupying. Soon after the government granted the land to ex-militia officers. We next hear of the Colonel as a merchant in his old home town of Boston, where he became the founder of the first large chain of American department stores. Two of his sons, U.C. and L.C. Hecklem (whose initials represented the Colonel's one bow to colonial patriotism), were generals in the American Civil War and implicated, by some accounts, in the assassination of President Abraham Lincoln. Redstone founded lucrative newspapers throughout the American frontier states and his son was the first major critic to recognize the importance of Henry James.

The Colonel's slaves back in Canada fared rather more badly. Despite the efforts of the imperial government, the provincial legislature passionately refused to consider effective remedial legislation to give them their freedom. There are reports of slaves from the Colonel's empire being sold throughout the 1830s in every year but one. But individual verdicts in the courts, based on defective legal procedures in the original enslavement, helped others. Finally, in the burst of long overdue reforms which Governor Sydenham pushed through about 1840, the last of the slaves was freed. Even at this late date there was a proposal that they should be sold to the Canada Company and the legislature grudgingly accepted their emancipation only on the agreement that they were to be barred from the vote for life.

Lampsden underwent a long period of decline after the Colonel's flight. With most of its buildings abandoned and with the land granted to the ex-militia officers, it began the free stage of its existence in a disordered state which ended only when two kinsmen of Bishop Strachan bought out the interest of the officers in the mid-1840s and began selling the land and the businesses to the former slaves. By the '60s the town was booming again and at least one of the children born in slavery became a Father of Confederation (see Chapter 5, *"Eminent Lampsdenites"*).

Today the memory of the slave-owning Colonel evokes a curious affection in Lampsden. The public park is named after him, as is the Founding Colonel Historical Society. One of his descendants, a Columbia University Professor and authority on the administration of Abraham Lincoln, often revisits the town. From his researches into family history we learn that the Colonel was no genuine Yankee but a defaulting bank clerk from Montreal who fled to Boston when the shots at Lexington signalled the opening of the American Revolution. His former employer and all his family disappeared mysteriously on a visit to Cuba about six months before Hecklem's return to Canada

C. CHRIS, *Lampsden (1960).*

UNDER THE BRICK

INTRODUCTION TO MY GOOD FRIEND
MR. TREEMORE'S NEW BOOK

It is an error to suppose that we did not have men and women of thought and learning in the Canadian forests in the first generation of settlement. Indeed, many a profound book was written in those days, often under circumstances of the most trying kind. Given the primitive conditions, such books seldom found a printer but enjoyed a celebrity in their neighbourhood for a few years or a few decades, being read again and again by attentive neighbours around the roaring log fires. Then, after their author's death, on the ignorant assumption that the manuscript was no longer wanted or no longer valuable, its well-thumbed pages were likely to be used by some ungrateful descendant for kindling fires.

A similar story could be told of our first generation of painters. And that works of sculpture of the greatest value were routinely chopped up for firewood as we know from the shocked testimony of Mrs. Moodie, who vainly attempted to rescue a series of 20 busts representing members of the now extinct Masqquila Indian tribe from being used for fuel at a school-master's sugar camp.

This remarkable pillage has been described by Ebbersob in his history of Canadian art as more far-reaching in its effects than the looting of the monasteries by Henry VIII or of the chateaux in the French Revolution. It is sad but perhaps not very surprising considering the human lust for destruction which history has so often had the sorrowful task of reporting. In the present pages we turn our thoughts to architecture, a field in which our first generation of settlers was as endlessly creative as in any other — and in which, it will delight and amaze many Canadians to learn, MANY OF THE FINEST ACHIEVEMENTS ARE STILL INTACT, if, as we shall see, not very accessible. But first, a few sad thoughts on what has been lost.

It is generally accepted that not one example survives of the most distinctive form of pioneer architecture, the log tower. We do, however, have several contemporary and near-contemporary drawings and paintings of log towers and they were often described by travellers and memoirists. The log tower was normally a square structure, three to six storeys high, being proportioned to rise at least one storey above the level of the tree tops of the surrounding forest. Anyone who has seen pictures of the Mayan pyramids rising above the jungle canopy will have an idea of what these log towers must have looked like. In the portion of the province north of Orangeville, the round log tower, resembling the medieval round towers of

Ireland, was occasionally found. In the round log tower the logs were placed in a vertical position, whereas in the more conventional square tower, they were horizontal. Altogether, in both forms, it would appear that about 1,000 log towers existed at one time or another in the province, with few being built after the outbreak of war in 1812.

Most authorities now concede that the purpose of the log towers was psychological rather than practical. Trapped in the interminable forest, cut off by its dense tangle of leaves and branches from the blue sky overhead, the pioneer could gain a limited sense of freedom for his family and himself by felling a few acres of the forest and letting in the air and sky and sunlight. But a larger open space was required if the pioneer was to feel himself more than a prisoner in the New World. This freedom he obtained by ascending the (normally square) spiral of the tower stairs and at last stepping out on the breezy upper platform and looking down on the forest which he and his descendants were destined one day to conquer. In addition, it may be freely conceded that the towers also sometimes served as lookout stations for forest fires and travellers or hostile Indians on the roads and waterways. The Clairseach tower (demolished 1825) seems to be the only recorded example of a tower being used for entombment. In this case the ground storey was packed with clay to provide a burial place for the powerful Ereseton family and the public ascended to the second storey (where the stairs began) by way of a log ramp.

"Excellence in architecture is more independent of size than of any other quality." (Napoleon) This rule worked to the advantage of the pioneers who, building principally log houses and similar small log structures, had to be masters of the small. And superb masters, from many testimonies that survive, is what some of them were.

This is perhaps hard to accept today because the log houses that survive have so often been put to ignominious uses — as hen houses, pig pens, woodsheds and the like. Viewing these sorry ruins today, with their misshapen logs, ill-cut joints, mouldering wood, makeshift 20th-century windows, slapdash mortaring and promiscuous patching with tar paper and bits of rusty tin, we may well suspect that the pioneers loved shiftless and unsightly building as much as ourselves.

Even the burdocks that grow tenaciously along the fieldstone foundations of such buildings, and in a wet season quickly balloon up to enclose the whole building as tightly as the Sleeping Beauty's palace, have become so closely associated in our minds with log cabins that we can hardly persuade ourselves that witless pioneers did not plant a garden of burdocks everytime they built a cabin. Burdocks are the most forceful of our everyday symbols of what the pioneer log cabin has become. For many people, it is to be feared, they are also symbols of what the pioneer log cabin always was.

But at this point we should ask ourselves the question — is it likely that the best the pioneers produced would be converted to such ignoble uses as hen houses and the like? In fact, there *was* a very different kind of pioneer log house. Exquisitely proportioned, elaborately carved with symbolic figures, masterpieces springing from profound thought and the most highly-cultivated taste, the pioneer log houses in their perfection were gems equal to the finest contemporary achievements of the European builders of cathedrals, palaces, country houses and public buildings. For the sake of convenience, architects have agreed to term these Ornamented Log Cabins (abbreviation: OLC). But where are these treasures of our early architecture today?

The purpose of the present book by Mr. Treemore is to describe in detail, with the aid of hundreds of drawings and photographs, four magnificent surviving Ornamented Log Cabins. All located in the Golden Triangle area of western Ontario, they have been carefully restored by their owners who have kindly consented to allow this study to be made and to allow documents and photographs in their possession to be reproduced. Dr. and Mrs. Fred Treebeam, Dr. and Mrs. A. Dilltz, Professor B. Ascoop and Sunglow Nuclear Corporation, the owners of these houses, deserve the most heartfelt thanks from all the readers of this book.

An appeal must be made to the public in connection with Mr. Treemore's research. It is well known that the fate of many of the early log cabins of Ontario was not to be demolished but to be covered over with brick to provide the conventional brick houses that had become fashionable by the 1830s. It is the purpose of my few remaining lines to emphasize two points. First, that thousands of OLCs are concealed beneath the brick of older houses in the Golden Triangle and other parts of Ontario. Secondly, that a government program should be undertaken, before further deterioration can take place under the damp, insect-collecting brick covering these houses, to persuade the owners of likely houses to strip them of their brick covering. The result in many cases will be the exposure for the first time in nearly a century and a half of treasures of pioneer art. In an age which has seen billions of dollars wasted in war and in such doubtful arts of peace as building the Concorde, it can hardly be argued that the expense involved in compensating owners whose houses, once stripped of part of their brick, prove to be commonplace log houses rather than the OLCs for which we are searching, can be regarded as excessive. We are not, in any case, facing a situation strictly measurable in money. We are concerned with the sole possibility of recovering our lost pioneer art on a large scale.

INTRODUCTION by J. DAN to P. TREEMORE, *Pioneer Masters (1968)*.

THE ONTARIO VOLCANO

It is a lie to say, as a recent textbook in geology does, that no one has ever seen an active volcano in Ontario. When my father cleared his farm in Prescott County, the deep marshy soil at the back of his 100-acre lot was so hot in one place that horses could not pass over it. Five years later the hot spot could be seen glowing red at night through the upper layers of soil. One day near the end of summer, about 8 o'clock on a Sunday morning, it collapsed to form a circular pit about 20 feet across, out of which thick smoke with sharp-grained ashes streamed for most of the following winter. A considerable amount of the ash, often mixed with snow, fell on Bytown (as it was then called) during the winter. I have some newspaper clippings about this.

In April there was an eruption of lava which pushed up like a big, flat bubble to the height of about a yard above the rim of the crater, then broke and poured out in all directions. It scorched about five acres of land and an arm of it ran into the South Nation River about two miles away.

But this was Nature's final stroke — for the time being at least. Within days after this eruption, the volcano reverted to total dormancy. It quickly filled up with ground water and today the shallow crater is used as a swimming hole and as a watering place for my brother's cattle. During the months that the volcanic activity was at its height, there was a continual sound like a sawmill steam engine loud enough to be heard over all the farm. I was nine years old when these events began on our farm and was an attentive, and I believe faithful, witness of them.

MARY ESTIL, *Farm Days (1886)*.

THE FUTURE AVERTED

Some years ago, in researching for my amusement the history of my native county, I read in some old memoirs that when the first pioneers came to the northeast section of this county, they did not find the venerable forest of giant trees which confronted the pioneers elsewhere, but a velvet lawn of luscious grass with violets, marsh marigolds, and other wild flowers stretching over the extent of what is now ten or a dozen farms. As a biologist this intrigued me, but on close examination of the area today (as fine an area of settled farms as this province can show) I could find no clues to this mystery. My work on the role of the carp in groundhog diet occupied most of my time for the next few years but I still found opportunities to search old records. I found first one, then another and finally about two dozen accounts, from widely separated parts of the province, of the existence, when the first settlers arrived, of these fine, treeless tracts — "lawn lands" as I soon began to call them. But all the time I was also looking for the clue that would help me to unravel the mystery. Therefore, when I learned that one of these lawn lands in the centre of Wellington County had remained virtually undisturbed since pioneer times, I lost no time in hurrying to visit it.

Almost my first efforts proved to be productive, for on digging the soil to a depth of about two feet, I found a thick layer of nearly microscopic white threads — a fungus hitherto unknown to science. As I determined by careful experiments over the next few years, this layer was invariably toxic to the roots of trees. Wherever the fungus spread, it created a lawn land. Several problems remained to be solved, however. Why had the fungus not spread, to turn the entire province of Ontario into as treeless a tract as the prairies? Did this fungus, in fact, explain the treelessness of the Canadian prairies? And why had it been found possible to grow shade trees and orchards (which can be seen in Arcadian abundance there today) on the lawn lands discovered by the pioneers, and for that matter, on the Canadian prairies?

For the answer to these problems, I am indebted to the dedicated labours of my parents, wife and children who worked as a research team under my direction in the years 1968 to 1970. The answer we found is that more than a dozen of the imported European weeds which afflict Canadian farmers and gardeners today, including burdock, Scotch thistle, dandelions, plantain and wild mustard, produce a toxin in their roots sufficient to destroy the fungus wherever they take root. It may be assumed that an ancient evolutionary struggle on the Eurasian continent has left these weeds, and perhaps many more not transplanted to our North American shores, equipped with the permanent apparatus for victory over the potent but highly susceptible fungus By the time the white settlers came to North America the slow-moving fungus had, over a period of thousands of years, deforested the prairies and had set up advance colonies in its eastward invasion of Ontario and Quebec. In due time — perhaps 500 years or more — Ontario would also have been denuded of trees. The one surviving patch of fungus I found was in a secluded forest grove, where European weeds had apparently never penetrated. When our experiments have been completed this patch too will be carefully destroyed by the planting of burdock, Scotch thistle and so forth. Having solved a remarkable problem in the history of Canada, my family of researchers and I hope now to investigate the possibility that the same process of fungus infestation may have created the treelessness of the Highlands of Scotland and the Sahara Desert in Africa.

DR. ROBERT CO, *When Local History and Global Biology Met (1972)*.

THE AGE OF CONFEDERATION

A DOG CHASING A CAT
WAS FOR SOME YEARS
A RARE SIGHT
IN PORTACH TOWNSHIP

I remember that in 1865 Gypsies came through our neighbourhood buying up all the dogs and cats they could get. The people were glad in those Spartan days to make a little money where they could and, except for a few particularly cherished favourites, the neighbourhood was quickly emptied of its old flourishing population of moggies and pooches. Like the rest of us, young and old, I wondered what the destination of these exiles was to be. Some said they were being taken for their fur, but this seemed inconsistent with the care with which one of our old neighbours, visiting Montreal, saw the Gypsies loading the live cats and dogs onto the trains at the rail yards.

I happened upon a newspaper item many years later which cleared up the whole mystery. As the American Civil War drew to a close, the demands by the war profiteers for luxurious restaurants in New York grew so unrestrained that many unscrupulous operators got into the game. They habitually served up cat and dog to their sensual but brutal clientele instead of the chicken, rabbit, lamb, veal, suckling pig and other delicate meats they supposed they were eating.

Strangely, our neighbourhood was observed to be remarkably free of rats and mice until the cat population had been built up again to its normal level, and then we had plagues of rats and mice as severe as ever before. It was supposed that a secret connection deeper than the casual eye can probe keeps the cat and rodent population in perfect balance with each other. It is certainly a common complaint of householders that when cats are eating them out of house and home, rats and mice are doing the same.

Many thought that people were healthier and that there were fewer deaths among the very young and the very elderly when the cat and dog populations were low.

P. COPELAND, *A Portach Township Boyhood (1923)*.

LITERARY PROGRESS

20 Nov. 1858. Drove to town with a load of grist. Wife lazy today so severely chided her before I set out. Returned to find her weeping. Soft-hearted woman. The children worked like demons all day, building the new barn.

16 Dec. 1858. First snowstorm of the season. Neighbour Chatson arrived at dawn. His wife had let the fire go out and he had to travel five miles through the snow to get some coals. Commiserated with him and persuaded my wife to tell him of some of her blunders to cheer him up. Found her sullen during the rest of day. In the end, had to strike her after supper.

23 Dec. 1858. After discussion at the store yesterday on whether our womenfolk are becoming enfeebled (as some clergymen believe) by the unhealthy cold of the Canadian climate, I conceived an idea of writing a book, *The Duties of the Backwoods Housewife*. Began work on it today and have filled almost 20 pages. It will be a welcome diversion this winter, especially when the wife and family are out cutting wood. Harley Brooke thinks he saw a robin last week — most unusual at this time of year.

28 March 1859. Manuscript completed today. Already I have made plans to sell the hogs to get cash to take ship to England to oversee the publication of this book.

London, 5 Sept. 1859

My dearest Lucinda,

You and all my family will be delighted to know that your husband and father is today the happiest man in London with the publication of his book, *The Duties of the Backwoods Housewife*. My publishers anticipate a large sale among those setting out for Canada, Yankeeland, New Zealand and Australia ... After I have seen France and Italy, I will return to you. With deepest love, your most affectionate &c., &c.

From the *Edinburgh Review*, January 1860: "*Among the flood of current books on emigration, we welcome a literary treasure which has come to us from the Canadian shore, in the form of a bulky yet wonderfully succinct manual,* The Duties of the Backwoods Housewife. *We hear that this book has so impressed the authorities of the Canada Company that its author will not be returning to Canada but will be taking up a lucrative position in this country.*"

London, 21 January 1862

Dear Sir,

Messrs. Sopwith and Sons present their compliments in returning to you the manuscript of your novel, *Deep in the Forests of Canada*. Under the present circumstances they regretfully cannot see their way clear to publishing it. Your observation about being unable to pay your hotel bill they beg leave to overlook, as not relating to a matter within the scope of their relations with an author they are personally unacquainted with.

The Times, London, 22 January 1862: *"The body of a heavily-bearded former Canadian settler was found floating today in the Thames ..."*

The Clairseach Reformer, 15 Sept. 1893: *"The Grand Old Lady of Clairseach Township, whose funeral took place yesterday to the accompaniment of more than 200 carriages and an attendance of young and old that has seldom been equalled in modern memory, had outlived her husband by more than 30 years ... Many of these were hard years for her but, by dint of unremitting labour, she made herself the proprietress of three flourishing farms and the chain of cheese factories which now make the good cheddar cheese which is one of the gustatory delights of the British householder and provides the golden stream of money which every year is the surest form of support for the industrious Clairseach farmer ... Her late husband, a man of literary interests, is said to have prepared or published a book on the duties of the pioneer housewife."*

From J. Blatz, *Literary History of Canada* (1970): *"One of the best Canadian books from the unpromising decade of the fifties is undoubtedly* The Duties of the Backwoods Housewife *(London, 1859) in which wit and humanity are united with an intimate knowledge of the customs of the frontier. J. Phostigam, in his thesis, 'Feminist Literature in Canada', seems conclusively to have proved that the man's name attached to the book is a pseudonym and that the real author was the early Kingston feminist writer, Alicia O'Kelly, who tragically disappeared with her husband Ned Murphy, the inventor of Murphy's Mechanical Mine Shaft Excavator, while exploring abandoned mine tunnels in Colorado in 1888."*

F. FOSSE, *A Family Treasure Chest (1963)*.

ASHES

We have seen, then, that the potash industry in Ontario reached its height between 1850 and 1880 and thereafter swiftly declined. But as the manufacture of potash had been, as we have seen, largely conducted out of the kitchens of pioneer housewives, this decline marked the end of the period when women had almost equal economic power in Ontario with men. With 1880 ended the era of the financially independent pioneer housewife, able to go into taverns on her own and be served and able to assert her views on the running of home, school and church. With 1880 began the era of the "lady", the waxen, cosseted and corseted, doll-like housewife with her neurotic

38

attachment to patent medicines, playing a role not unlike that of the females in the contemporary Turkish seraglio.

In their valuable study of the expenditure of energy in housework, *Miles and Distance*, the sociologists Bahn and Reeper argue that where N represents units of housework energy and X represents productivity,

$$\frac{X}{N}\sqrt{2}.5 \times \text{current cash value of a farm}$$

If this is correct it may be further calculated, in terms of Mohnekopf's standard table of economically productive ratios, that the dramatic increase in foreclosures on farm mortgages after 1880 was both a result of the decline of the woman-dominated potash trade and a powerful factor in the enslavement of the backwoods housewife. She now stood stripped of the last shreds of the economic independence which had formerly been her shield against the predatory urban capitalist, of which her husband, father, brothers, sons, uncles and other male relatives were the local types and representatives.

K. RON, "Potash" (thesis, 1974).

ANYONE HERE CALLED RUPERT JONES?

I don't know whether it is generally known that a whole orphanage of 600 boys, all called Rupert Jones, of which my great-grandfather was one, was brought to Canada about 80 years ago. The founder and master of the orphanage was Adolphus M'Ruprecht, who is well known among Dickensians (my nephew is a well-known Dickens collector) as the model for Mr Mirabel, the sadistic philanthropist in Charles Dickens' lost novel about cannibalism, *Little Gorgeous*. Destroyed in the great fire at the Adolfosso Hotel the day before its author was to present it to the publisher, this novel is said to have been one of Dickens' finest. M'Ruprecht was later sentenced to life imprisonment for stealing 10 shillings from one of his little charges called of course, Rupert Jones. When it was discovered, years later, that the theft had been committed by another boy, also called Rupert Jones but not apparently one of the orphans M'Ruprecht was pardoned and finished his life as a gardener at Balmoral. If this criminal mishap had not occurred it is believed, such was his one-time fame, that M'Ruprecht and his 600 orphans would have been included among the figures on the Albert Memorial in Kensington Gardens, London.

ANYONE HERE CALLED RUPERT JONES?

Perhaps he had some presentiment of his coming misfortunes when he accompanied the 600 Rupert Joneses to Canada. My great-grandfather, who was a great favourite of his, remembers him saying in a musing way, shortly after the boat docked at Quebec, that the United States, particularly west of the Mississippi, offered a security an honest man could no longer trust to find in Old England.

I have always thought that his influence in Canada has been underestimated due partly to the fact that practically all his boys changed their names to more distinctive forms shortly after their old friend and master had taken a sorrowful farewell of them and returned, lamenting, to Britain. I think that some concept of publicizing the effect of his pedagogical theories — by bringing before the public hundreds of examples of what a boy could become, all the examples marked out by their identical names — was the real cause of his strange decision to call all his boys Rupert Jones. After swearing me to secrecy, my great-grandfather in his old age showed me an almost complete list of the boys with the names they had assumed after shedding that of Rupert Jones. I was astonished to find on it the names of several of the most distinguished Canadians of the day, including that of our then Prime Minister.

M'RUPRECHT RUPERT-JONES, *A Family Garland (1930)*.

MARX IN TORONTO

In the long drawn out attempt to found Lake Ontario University in Toronto, 1865 was a heady year. Then professors were actually hired, a few classes were assembled and lectured to and fund raising was pushed with renewed vigour to supply a campus and a building. In that year, too, Toronto had one of its most distinguished, although at this time not well known, visitors in the form of Karl Marx, who came in the hopes of obtaining the Professorship of Moral Philosophy at the new university. He is described by Mr. George Hopewell, a Toronto businessman who interviewed him on behalf of the Board of Governors, as *"a soft-spoken old German rascal, with many strange gaps in his logic, but with excellent references from a Manchester businessman, F. Engels, with whom my family has done much business."* Marx himself described Toronto as "a loathsome puritanical-hypocritical catchpool for all the urban and rural horrors of the Old World and the New", but as *"much better"* than Berlin, Ontario, where his nephew, a schoolteacher, pulled strings to get him the opportunity to deliver a sparsely attended lecture at the Mechanics Institute on Lord Palmerston and the Eastern Question.

As usual, during his few weeks in Canada he was indefatigably busy. His acerbic comments on the Confederation scheme, sent to Sir John A. Macdonald and to be found among Sir John A.'s papers in the National Archives in Ottawa, seem to have resulted in several last-minute changes in the structure of the Canadian Senate. He also compiled his manuscript, *"Inhuman Working Conditions in Factories Owned by Prominent Humanitarians in Toronto and Berlin, Canada"*, one of his least popular works, but which tends to reappear in a flurry of new editions and new translations whenever the world communist movement takes one of its sharp turns to the left.

In the end, we do not know whether Marx was offered the position at the university or not. All references to it fade out of his correspondence by the late spring of 1866. George Brown of the *Globe* described the recently published *Das Kapital* Vol. I, of 1867, as being *"by the fellow who left the unpaid bills at Mrs. Molly's boarding house at the time of the university fiasco."* Six months later the bills were paid by Mrs. Molly Breacon's brother-in-law the Toronto Chief of Police. An astonishing connection? Did Marx's visit to Toronto have a secret history of which we know nothing?

N. WENTWORTH, *Extinct and Dormant Universities of Ontario (1965).*

CRACKERBOX HOMELAND

It seems not to be well known that the crackerbox house, so long the symbol of rural Ontario, was first extensively used in this province in the Freddyville farming community in the 1840s. Its popularity there is said to be owing to a young architect from the United States who returned to his parents' Freddyville home with tuberculosis and succeeded in converting his neighbours to this new form of building before he died.

As late as a generation ago the traveller to this community was often moved to ask the reason not only for the extraordinary number of crackerbox houses, but why they were never painted and never had any trees about them. The recent revival of appreciation of this typical building form of Old Ontario has also revived awareness that, as originally planned by its American and Canadian founders, the crackerbox house was to stand on treeless, preferably flat, land and was never under any circumstances to be painted. But as the form became the favourite of a mass public of little education, these austere rules were often forgotten. Painted crackerbox houses (this form is often referred to as *"relaxed crackerbox"*) began to appear and some crackerbox houses were not only painted but had trees about them. To the eye of the connoisseur rural Ontario was long to present a painful mingling of strict observance and various degrees of disregard for

43

or softening of the rules. But it appears that in Freddyville, perhaps in deference to the memory of the young architect and his tragic fate, the authentic traditions were observed in their most unbending form for a long time. It was only in the vandalistic wave of rebuilding promoted by post-Second World War prosperity that this nursery of the crackerbox house in Ontario was so effectively gutted that the recently proposed schemes to reconstruct the entire community as a National Heritage Spot must be dismissed as hopelessly utopian.

ATWIN AND CREEP, *Visual Adventures (1975)*.

THE QUORDSMILL CONFERENCE

Was our village the place where Canadian Confederation began? Strong evidence suggests that it was. In 1862 and 1863 groups of masked men were regularly seen entering the back room of the municipal hall, where mysterious meetings lasted long into the night. It was sometimes dawn before they dispersed. They always rode away in the direction of Toronto. Sometimes they spoke in English and sometimes in French. Angus McCairdeen, the precentor, more than once heard them speak in Gaelic. Once, when a mask slipped, Miles Carter the blacksmith, who lived across from the hall, recognized the face of his political hero George Brown. His sister and housekeeper, Miss Carter the milliner, on no less than six separate occasions espied the remarkable nose of Sir John A. Macdonald.

Preceding the Charlottetown Conference by more than a year, these meetings at Quordsmill must properly constitute the QUORDSMILL CONFERENCE, the first of the *four*, not three, conferences that led up to Confederation. It is said that Sir John A. was questioned about this matter later in life by our Member of Parliament, Sir Alexander Tradmill. Sir John, who was going through one of his periodic phases of ill health at this time, was crouched low over a hot glass of brandy and at first hardly seemed to understand the question. But at last, when its meaning had been made abundatly clear to him, he responded in a very loud voice with the statement that much could not be told at present, but that if the good people of Quordsmill would bide their time, they would see full justice done to the name of their good town. This has not been done to this day. It is hoped that the simple facts stated here will begin to remedy an injustice.

JAMES SMITHNESS, *Quordsmill (1920)*.

ENTREPRENEURS

FIGURES

No plaque marks the spot but one will be placed shortly. To date only a few lumps of masonry in the shallow, weed-clotted, slow-running waters of the Season River about half a mile south of the village of Burnetville Station mark the site of the pioneer mill of Jonathan Burnet, one of the fathers of Canadian technology. Burnet was one of the Scots who served as engineers in the Russian armies of the 18th century. He settled about 1798 in this part of the Canadian forest, where he was soon the prospering owner of a large grist mill designed in accordance with principles he had observed in use in the grist mills of Lithuania. Ever an enterprising man, when leisure had crowned his labours he returned to the mathematical studies that had occupied his youth in Edinburgh. Combining these with his knowledge of the most advanced technology of the day, he soon had in operation, powered by his mill, a large calculator which, we are told, could add, subtract, multiply and divide and extract square roots. Occupying the large room above the mill stones, it is said to have been four feet by six feet by three feet and to have been so heavy that when his son-in-law sold it to Egerton Ryerson in 1852 it took four oxen to carry it in the largest cart of the neighbourhood to the nearest dock on Lake Ontario.

A kind of giantism seems to have seized Burnet after this and we find his second machine, which could extract cube roots, occupied a three-storey tower and needed a second water wheel to help power it. A third machine, described in a small book published anonymously in New York in 1811 as *"designed to perform all the mathematical functions of which the most advanced human mathematicians are capable"*, was completed shortly before the miller's death in 1825. Steel plate engravings in De Villiers' well-known travel memoirs show the two massive towers, one on each side of the stream, which housed the last and most massive of Burnet's inventions. The towers were seized by rebels in 1837, probably at the instigation of Burnet's son who was a noted radical, and were burned by Sir Francis Bond Head's troops in 1838. They appear to have been empty of all the calculating apparatus by this time and, according to a tradition which still survives in the neighbourhood of Burnetville Station, the mechanism had been bought by an Italian general in the service of Ranjit Singh, the last great maharajah of the Sikh kingdom of the Punjab. It had been packed in 100 packing crates and transported down the St. Lawrence to Quebec City and from there to India. Some parts of the mechanism are said to have been seen in Afghanistan by a Scottish general, one of Burnet's kinfolks, during the British invasion of that country in 1879. If even a few parts of this mechanism could now be located, we would be in a better position to guess at the true scope of Burnet's achievement.

R. HANSARD, *The Miller of Burnetville Station (1981).*

A TECHNOLOGICAL PIONEER

There are prosperous farms, towns and cities today in this province where 100 years ago there were only swamps and forests. For this we give the pioneers who cleared the land credit, and after them the farmers and businessmen who laboured decade after decade to give us prosperity. But among this multitude of people who worked for our good, I fear some have been unworthily lost from sight. It is for this reason that I take leave to revive before the public the reputation of my great-grandfather Samuel Divers, the founder of penology in this province. Working as a freelance, never on a government payroll, a stout businessman every inch of the way, he did not leave as many state records as many persons of smaller achievement.

How laws were enforced and crime was punished in pioneer times is a mystery to many today, even among those well read in our pioneer lore. It is true that there was less serious crime then than in these desperate days, but the pioneers were people of such severe morals that much that would not pass for crime today was remorselessly punished as such then. Yet anyone who will scrutinize the face of early Ontario will notice how few and how small the recorded prisons were!

What then was done with prisoners? The answer is that imprisonment was widely regarded not as work for the public sector but as work for the private sector, and the private sector in this case meant my good great-grandfather Samuel Divers. As the inventor of barbed wire, which he found to be in little demand among the farmers and cattlemen of those days, who had no particular objection to letting their cattle wander over the neighbouring forests or, for that matter, over their neighbours' hay and grain fields, he sought a new application for his invention and found an ideal one in its utility for the enclosure of prisoners. By 1810 he had established throughout the province a network of barbed wire camps, in which the local authorities paid him 2d per head to maintain prisoners. He calculated that the lowest sum at which a prisoner could be sustained bodily was 4d but, by steady application to the productive work which was intended to be a cure for the restlessness and addiction to vice which had brought him to this place, he could earn enough to make up the difference and a little more.

47

Sawing and splitting firewood for the growing towns was one of the occupations of the prisoners. During the War of 1812 complete secrecy was imposed on the operation of the camps. I know, however, from family tradition, that a large new camp was opened for the duration of the war in the security of the Melancthon Swamp in western Ontario. My great-grandfather's fee was reduced to 1d per day, but it would appear that even under these reduced circumstances he made a passable living during the war. In a government report of 1818 we read that there were at this time 48 of the camps scattered throughout the Province of Upper Canada, from a few miles west of the Quebec border in Glengarry County to a sandspit near Kincardine on the shore of Lake Huron. The large camp which served the needs of York (Toronto) was located to the north of the city on a Crown Reserve lot near the hamlet of Thornhill. In the same year the reformer Robert Gourlay was briefly imprisoned in the Frontenac County camp, which served mainly the needs of Kingston. My great-grandfather's empire seems to have peaked by the mid-1820s. Increasingly thereafter we hear of the state providing its own facilities for the holding of prisoners.

The close political alliance my great-grandfather unwarily formed with William Lyon Mackenzie seems finally to have spelled the end for his camps by turning the authorities against him, and by 1832 he was a bankrupt. The last camp, run by this time by a syndicate of money-lenders drawn from among his creditors, must have closed by 1841. By this time my great-grandfather had gone to the United States, where he served for the rest of his life as the secretary-treasurer of a New York foundation for homeless immigrants.

MYRTLE COPS, *A Family Chronicle (1891)*.

MINERAL SPRINGS

Ontario has its share of the mineral springs which once made places like Bath and Mallow famous but alas, our province came along so late in the mineral spring game that it was never possible to interest a wide public in what it saw as the preoccupation of a bygone age. Nevertheless, here and there these spring flourished, and one such founded the fortunes of our town which, for about 20 years in the 1840s and '50s, attracted fashionable visitors and hopeful invalids from all over Canada West and the northeastern United States. The discoverer, proprietor and medical consultant of the spring was Dr. Richard Hutenglass, whose bulky, cylindrical figure, surmounted by a bushy, buttercup-yellow beard and crimson top hat, can still be studied in the fine oil painting in our public library.

In researching the history of the spring I of course tested the water for mineral content. To my surprise the famous mineral spring showed no mineral content at all except for a very small amount of that very common substance calcium carbonate, usually found in well water. At first I thought that over the course of years the nature of the water had changed. But the chance discovery of the existence, in the 1830s, of an American firm which specialized in the supply of barrels of powdered mineral to be dumped weekly in springs to make them *"mineral"* set me thinking. Could Dr. Hutenglass have salted our spring? Hardly, because the American company had gone into bankruptcy before our spring was discovered and had never, apparently, reopened. But who was the proprietor of the American company? None other, I discovered on examining its papers, than Dr. Hutenglass himself. We must assume that after the failure of his American company he fled to Canada and the man who once essayed to help others exploit a network of fraudulent springs was now content to nurture fame and fortune. Dr. Hutenglass must be judged to have done rather well at this, for he ended up as a large landowner in the area and a Professor of Physic at one of our early medical schools. Apparently the good doctor was himself a believer in mineral springs, if genuine, for he was taking the cure at Baden Baden when he died in 1883.

The university in which he taught has kindly made his private papers available to me and, although they contain no secrets about spurious mineral springs, they do show him preoccupied, near the end of his life, with a very curious geological problem, namely that of how to create a hot spring by chemical means. I find from newspaper reports that a hot spring was alleged to have been discovered near Walkerton, Ontario in 1880, in an area where Hutenglass had extensive investment in farm mortgages, but I have been unable to trace either the exact location of the spring or any other particulars about it.

R. MORTON, *History of Gluten Springs (1963).*

THE BIRTH OF THE HALDIMAND PAPERS

My father was a professional writer when there were few such in Canada. As you can easily imagine, he had to struggle to make a living. We were a family of 10 in our little stone house beside the harbour in Kingston. In December, just before the lake freezes over, Kingston goes through its period of most stinging cold. The air then is like a bath of ice water. No other cold I have ever known penetrates to the bone like the cold of a Kingston December. When it happened, as it often did, that Pa was short of money, we couldn't afford enough firewood to see us through those days of piercing cold. Some of my most poignant early memories are of huddling under piles of pillows, blankets and buffalo robes with my little brothers in the front room of our house while, by the dim light of the candles on his desk, my father wrote and wrote and wrote.

Though the sufferings of his family were often cruel my father once informed me, in the strictest words a father can use to a son he loves, that he had only once been led by them into an act of dishonesty. He added with the same firmness of language that if I were ever to write a memoir of him, I should on no account omit, but for dear conscience' sake report, that he had been guilty of this act but not to state what it was, even if I should come to know. *"What I did,"* he said, *"if posterity cannot find out for itself, it were better off never knowing. But I was paid £175 for it."*

FREDERICK RENTZ, *A Kingston Boyhood (1920).*

My father was a wild Irish landowner of the sort described by Maria Edgeworth in *Castle Rackrent*. Long before the potato famine and the Land League ruined the Irish landlords, our family was in debt. Through my father's continual course of celebrations, gambling, drinking, hunting and dissipations of the sort the Victorians called venereal, his debts became mountainous. Under these circumstances every financial relief, however small, became welcome as a means of staving off a few more of his creditors for even a few days. It was while he was in these dire circumstances that there fell into his hands (by what means I know not, but I fear that among the possible explanations the plunder of a wealthy orphan to whom he had become the guardian must not be excluded) the private papers of a great Swiss general who had been an administrator in the colony of Canada for some years towards the end of the 18th century. They contained, it seemed, a pretty full account of the settlement in Canada, under Haldimand's direction, of some people called the United Empire Loyalists. Almost immediately the British Museum offered to buy these papers for a goodly sum. But no sooner had the telegram containing the offer reached my father's castle than, in one of the riotous wakes which my father positively encouraged his servants to keep in his vast and filthy kitchens, a drunken footman tossed the bundles of manuscript into the fireplace to heat some wine.

EDITOR'S NOTE: The Haldimand Papers are one of the main historical sources for the early history of English Canada. The originals are in the British Museum, London, England, but transcripts and microfilm copies are in the National Archives in Ottawa.

My father's younger brother Jack, who was out of gaol by this time and about to leave for Canada to take up an official position in the justice department which he had got through our family connection with Lord Northmoreland, immediately proposed as a solution that my father should ask the British Museum to allow him to delay the sale of the papers for one year so that he might peruse them himself before parting with them forever. During this year he, Jack, might easily find some contemptible hack in the colony to rewrite (indeed, to reinvent) the Haldimand Papers completely. My father objected that their cousin, the Reverend Mr. M'Ree, the Church of Ireland clergyman of the district who most Sundays had no congregation in his church and often waited for weeks before he had an opportunity to use the sermon he had written, could do the job as well and without the delay necessarily occasioned by the distance from Canada. But Jack said no, the job must be done by someone who knew the Canadian geography and who knew the story of the United Empire Loyalists — whatever they were — that for this nothing but a native of the Canadas would answer. Besides, Reverend Mr. M'Ree was an honest man and would balk at a job that no one but a villain would undertake. Plenty of such could be found in the colonies, where gentlemen and honest men were alike unknown.

All this was done as the ingenious brother proposed and a few months later he wrote back to say (and I have his letter in front of me) that he had found a broken tradesman of blacker villainy than any of the cutpurses of Dublin, who lived in a little stone house by the harbour in Kingston (the town where the Lady Patrickson's brother stabbed his mistress). This man professed to be an author but was half-mad with poverty and had leapt at the opportunity to take on this new task for £175. He was now actually at work on it and in six months would have a new set of Haldimand Papers written, better than the originals.

The broken tradesman was as good as his word. My father received the Haldimand Papers and duly sold them to the British Museum, where they rest to this day without, so far as I know, any creature ever questioning their authenticity, though they are as much an invention as anything in Grimm's *Fairy Tales* or in Lord Morley's life of that Sinn Fein rogue Gladstone.

COLONEL H. HURRY, *Fox Hunting Memoirs (1922)*.

... a few steps further on we come to a large asphalted parking lot. Full of cars by day, by night it is crossed only by the occasional mugger hurrying to more affluent parts of the city. On this lot formerly stood a picturesque jumble of stone buildings — shops, houses, stables, and among the houses that of Murdoch Rentz, who was one of the earliest professional writers in Canada. Rentz is now believed on fairly good evidence to have forged the famous Haldimand Papers. Computer studies now under way at Queen's University are expected soon to definitively confirm or deny this charge.

Rentz also wrote a once-famous history of the early years of English Canada, but since one of his principal sources was the Haldimand Papers, of which he may himself have been the author, the standing of this work too is gravely in doubt. Curiously, in the demolition that made way for the present parking lot, it was discovered that the site had originally been one of the earliest Loyalist cemeteries. Several of the well-preserved tombstones, with their inscriptions turned inwards, had been built into the Rentz fireplace.

Gilder's Guidebook to Kingston, 12th ed., (1981).

L'ALBERTVILLE

Almost 15 years before the late Mr. Bell made his successful experiments with the telephone at Brantford, Ontario, my father had a telephone system operating in the little rural community of L'Albertville, about an hour's train ride northwest of Cornwall. Its central apparatus was a large black, cast-iron globe about 20 feet across, very much like an oversized diving bell and suspended on a log framework at a height of about 10 feet above the ground. From the holes in this globe the wires radiated out to the homes and businesses of the community. Down on the ground a wood-burning steam engine, connected to the globe by a belt, provided the necessary power. This device remained in use in L'Albertville till the death of my father in 1899. Afterwards no one who presented himself to work the system had his knack of making repairs so the community reluctantly went over to Mr. Bell's system, then in general use. My father's system had the advantage that no one could listen in on other people's conversations. The L'Albertville people, though fiercely proud of my father's invention, thought themselves deprived by being without an amusement that their neighbours in nearby communities enjoyed and liked to visit houses where they could listen in on the phone.

Father also believed that if it would be possible, by a multitude of tiny channels, to feed steam power to all the different parts of a clockwork mechanism, it would be possible to transmit moving pictures of people and scenes to every house, either for purposes of communication or for purposes of a pleasant and wholesome family entertainment. Father put the design of his mechanism on paper but never solved the problem of how to reconcile the force of the steam with the delicacy of the necessary machinery with its almost infinite number of small moving parts.

MRS. J. BOSTON, *L'Albertville (1922).*

A PIONEER OF RESEARCH

Among our townsmen in the 1890s was "Skulls" Benson, who was one of the first researchers in Ontario to apply archaeology to the study of local history. His chosen life's work was to reconstruct in its entirety the story of what kind of clothing our pioneer ancestors wore. One of his beliefs was that this could only be done successfully by opening pioneer graves and examining such buckles, buttons and other objects, including fragments of cloth, as had survived. His notes on his grave openings and his collections, including his scrapbooks of more than 500 samples of pioneer fabrics, are of great value to scholars. Unfortunately his family, which was very high and mighty and overvalued its social position, objected to what they regarded as disgraceful violations of the dead on the part of a relative who would not work and had him confined to an asylum. I sometimes used to visit him there. He died in 1926.

R. JONES, *Bensontown Remembered (1948)*.

REVENGE

The old-style newspaper editor, especially in the small towns, led an exciting life but one of self-denial. It is no exaggeration to say of many of these fine old gentlemen that they were horsewhipped at least once at every general election and never ate meat except when they were in jail. One editor known to your grandfather grew so disgusted by the rough treatment meted out to him by the local people when they slaughtered his chicken flock one night that he went to Montreal and returned with a large sum of money, procured by what means no one could ever determine, and set himself up as a money-lender.

Over the next 20 years he had mortgages on at least half the farms of his county and foreclosed on so many of them that it was said nobody ever harassed his neighbours as mercilessly as he. He brought up all his numerous sons as lawyers except one, and him he placed in his business to carry on the exactions into another generation. He married his daughter to the son of a notorious family of thieves and confidence men and established the younger generation of them in his town to prey on the people. From about 1900 onwards it was observed that the population of the area declined swiftly. Young couples refused to have families and the young, old and middle-aged flocked out together. But relief was at hand. The journalist's son, having unwisely transferred his interests from farm mortgages to the stock market, was wiped out in the 1929 Crash and after that all the family left the countryside where they had been a scourge since the days of s's that looked like f's.

PETER PROSTER, *Memoirs of a Family of Printers (n.d.).*

A RISING FAMILY

The railway came to Crepton Township in 1882 following a line between the Great Marsh and the Crepton Hills, where old Mr. Crepton had established his farms, mills and the town plot of the village of Crepton. He had six sons and the eldest, Malcolm, who is commemorated by the Crepton Range and Crepton City in Montana, was trained as a school-teacher. Finding the tug of commerce stronger than the charms of pedagogy he established, in Crepton and the adjacent townships, the first chain of general stores in Ontario. The second son, Frederick, organized the four remaining Crepton brothers into the firm of Crepton & Co., Stocks, Bonds, and Mortgages. It is no exaggeration to say that such was their enterprise that few farm properties in the entire county did not pass through their hands in the next 30 years. John was situated in the northwest corner of the county, Alexander at the southeast, and Frederick, Murphy and Oswald were located along an axis drawn from the northeast to the southwest corner of the county in such a way as to divide the axis into equal portions. In this way the brothers dispersed themselves as evenly as possible over the territory they faithfully served.

All the brothers married early and had large families (see Genealogical Tables). Their sons were settled in business and professional practices throughout the provinces of Ontario, Quebec and Manitoba. Their daughters were dispersed in good marriages to husbands of means and enterprise throughout the Dominion. One of these daughters married Sir Joshua Rix of Toronto and Montreal, the clothing magnate, whose textile factories provided welcome jobs for thousands of grateful immigrant women in the early decades of this century. Another married the real estate entrepreneur Elmer Sides, whose title as the Tenement King was as well known in Halifax and Vancouver as in Montreal, Toronto and Winnipeg. It is to be hoped that someday an enterprising young Canadian author will uncover and chronicle the history of these remarkable sons and daughters of Crepton Township in the exhaustive manner their achievements deserve.

Malcolm, the eldest of the original Crepton brothers and in many ways the founder of the family fortunes, fled to the United States in 1911 in mysterious circumstances in the company of two chambermaids and died in Hawaii in 1935. Frederick and John died in the influenza epidemic in 1918. Their splendid tomb, with its twin towers of polished Crepton Township granite, was destroyed by dynamite in the following year by a roving band of ex-servicemen. The graves of these businessmen, repeatedly desecrated by vandals (said to be the sons of local farmers) over the ensuing 20 years, are sadly without a marker today. Alexander, Murphy and Owald became recluses as the years passed. Drawing together, after death had stripped them of their wives, into a single mansion in the village of Crepton, they saw the prosperity of the village wither in the Great Depression and were sometimes to be seen, aged, ragged and careworn figures, slipping through the half-light of dawn or dusk to the post office or the general store. The sleet storms of 1941 proved too much for their enfeebled constitutions and pneumonia carried them all off within a single month. Today the site of their house is occupied by the municipal swimming pool.

Readers, and especially young readers, do you understand what I have said? Our prosperity today is based on their solid achievements. In the words of Susannah Kriep,

> What matters they have neither
> Tombs nor flowers
> Their gatherings, so substantial,
> Aren't they ours?

M. BOYD, *Crepton Man (1964)*.

THE LOST MANUSCRIPT

It is with sorrow that I bring my history to perhaps the saddest event ever to befall Uniono'fortyoneton – the murder of Tommy Mean Fomhair, which involved the destruction of his vast manuscript history of U'ton. The story is known too well to residents of our town to need more than a cursory retelling here. Tommy was found lying slumped over his work table with more than 40 wounds from a knife in his back. In the grate were the ashes of his manuscript – the only intact portions, which served to identify the rest, being some spots and patches which escaped incineration because they were drenched with the poor lad's blood.

The burning of the manuscript strangely paralleled Tommy's own work habits. For his sources he had the immense collection of papers on the history of the town collected over 70 years by his great-uncle Senator Mean Fomhair. The Senator had directed that these papers were to be used by some competent hand to prepare a suitable history of U'ton, but that as the manuscript of the history was completed, page by page, the source material was to be dropped into the fire. It was known that on the very night that Tommy died he had planned to finish the history and drop the last of his great-uncle's papers into the flames. Since none of the said papers were ever found, it has been conjectured that either Tommy did finish the history before his death, or that the murderer destroyed the historian, the manuscript and the few remaining papers together. The murder remains unsolved to this day and I have heard someone say that it resembles the three or four mysteries which Sherlock Holmes found totally unsolvable.

R. McDEED, *Our Town (1940).*

A PATENT MEDICINE KING

In its early years the most eminent citizen of Dultonville was Asof Dulton, the Roan Horse-Goldenrod Patent Medicine King. He had studied herbal cures among Indians in the United States but traced the turning point in his career to the day when he sold his strawberry roan horse to Gypsies near Collingwood for the secret of the curative powers of goldenrod. When I let my mind run back to the country stores of my youth, I see at once a shelf full of coal-black, sharply rectangular bottles with a red horse and a spray of goldenrod on them. That was the famous goldenrod elixir, product and pride of Dultonville.

Asof Dulton was a businessman who saw far beyond the narrow sphere of the production of his factories. Indeed, we may go further and say that he was the kind of businessman who in his practices laid out broad highways for others to follow. Accordingly, even before his plant had gone into operation, he had practically founded the modern advertising agency. He employed a team of ex-schoolteachers, male and female and mainly from the backwoods schools. They occupied an office next to his own where they sat around an oval table all day and wrote advertising copy with which he flooded the press of the United States and Canada. It has been calculated that one of these copywriters alone, Dave Portach the poet, wrote more than 50,000 personal testimonials from satisfied users of the elixir.

Among these the most famous was that from the Mountain Girl in Tennessee who swallowed half a dozen baby snakes while drinking water from a mountain pool. The snakes grew, forming a churning knotted mass in her stomach. Her screams, as the snakes tore at the delicate linings of her stomach, were terrible. Fortunately an elderly missionary told her of the goldenrod elixir. She drank some and was immediately cured.

The old folks in Dultonville had a curious story to tell about this elixir. Till about 1888, they alleged, the elixir could stop nearly any disease, even diphtheria, smallpox, tuberculosis and cancer, in its tracks. But after that time the medicine's effectiveness faded. The delicate Wisteria sisters, who had been dying one by one of T.B. till they began dosing themselves with the elixir, now began to die again. First Emilia, then Scotia, Florence and so forth, one or two per year, till poor Esmeralda breathed her last in 1896 and their house, one of the historic mansions of Dultonville, was sold to the county to serve as a jail. Dulton himself, it was observed, sent his children away to boarding schools in the United States to conceal that they no longer enjoyed their old joyous immunities but had turned sickly and were grinding their way for the first time through the usual childhood afflictions of chickenpox, whooping cough, mumps, pinkeye, impetigo and so forth. Oldtimers speculated that the formula sold to Dulton by the Gypsies had not been perpetually valid but limited to the horse's lifetime.

Dulton at this time almost wholly abandoned his supervision of the factory. Leaving its operation to the foremen, he scoured the countryside of Western Ontario and northern New York State with six wagonloads of fine horses accompanying him everywhere. He returned to the factory one Saturday night in 1897 and shot himself in his office. His sons and brothers, none of whom lived long, ran the factory after him, expanding it almost yearly up to the beginning of the Great Depression. The sales of the elixir climbed year by year and the wealth of the family grew immense. Their long, florid, and, if the word is not inappropriate, ornate wills in which they left everything in intricate bequests to each other fascinated the local people. But nobody from Dultonville used the elixir anymore. Out of principles of loyalty everyone concealed from outsiders that the elixir had been rejected in its own town. It was sorely missed I can tell you when the influenza epidemic swept through the town in 1918 and 1919. The medicine had a last revival of prosperity in the 1950s, but the factory closed in the '60s when a carcinogen scare destroyed its market. Today Dultonville, soon to be a suburb of Toronto, is without an industry.

R. DEPHAS, *Dultonville (1975)*.

... AND COUNTRY DOCTORS

All knew and loved the dear old country-doctors. Nevertheless, it must be admitted that among these heroic figures there were some whose training and perceptions were inadequate and who, after a night of driving through storm and flood or forests on fire, would cheerfully misdiagnose and prescribe incorrectly for the case at hand. It was this heroism that marked Dr. W. Arzt, the founder of our town. It was also this low degree of medical skill that also marked Dr. Arzt, founder of our town.

It was perhaps this very bright man's recognition of his own limitations, rather than love or a desire to buy over a powerful professional rival, that caused him to marry Mrs. Trolly, the herb doctor. Thereafter they rode together on their errands of mercy. Dr. Arzt provided the larger share of the heroism and Mrs. Trolly provided the medical lore.

Years after their deaths a researcher discovered that Arzt was an impostor, having never attended medical school at all, while Mrs. Trolly had studied medicine at a leading medical school in Germany at a time when women were permitted to attend classes but not to take degrees or practice their profession.

This fine old medical couple are buried at Rolland's Corners in a private cemetery on a farm they acquired by foreclosing a mortgage on the first settler, and where they entertained each of the first six prime ministers of Canada.

R. BOBSCH, *Arztlands and Rolland's Corners (1951)*.

BLACK NELSON THE BURNER

MADAME PRESIDENT, LADIES AND GLENTLEMEN:

Several of the most remarkable people in the province have been born in this quiet old town but tonight I want to tell you about my researches into a character I am sure you have all heard of, Black Nelson the Burner. Black Nelson was born about 1850 to a couple who kept a shebeen on the edge of town, about where the Carnation Milk Plant stands now. He died in 1930 in a Home for Distressed Gentlefolks founded in Toronto by the millionaire gambler, Frederick Concert. His schooling was brief so we may say that for most of the years between those dates he was a wanderer over the face of Ontario.

My research into this gentleman has been long, as some of you know, (*polite applause from audience*) and I think I have been able to establish for him a greater – as my sons at the university would say – social significance. (*polite laughter from several ladies and gentlemen at front of audience*)

What everybody knows about him is that he sometimes set fires. The burning of his father's shebeen when he was 12 years old, the burning of the Manse a few years later, the fires at Kingston, Berlin and Collingwood – they all come to mind. But as I delved into his history I made the interesting discovery that it was possible, for most of Nelson's life, to establish a record of his journeyings across the face of the province. That wonderful diary kept by our fellow townsman, the late Alexander Orboldt, is full of notices of Nelson's comings and goings and of rumours where he was last seen. Miss Repp's letters, to which I have been given access by her great-niece, also help – some people say Conan Doyle's Sherlock Holmes was modelled on Miss Repp. (*audience: Ha, Ha*) With these splendid guides to direct me I next went to the local newspapers and found that they filled out still further my data on his wanderings. I found that I had on my hands a growing pack of file cards listing practically day by day where Black Nelson was travelling. (*polite gasps of amazement from audience*) But I also began to find that this itinerary (*laughter and protest from fun-loving members of audience: "What's an itinerary?" "Give us fellows from the sticks a break, eh?" &c.*) coincided remarkably with a list of serious fires. Seldom a week went past in which four or five major fires did not spring up in towns where The Burner was travelling. My facts are necessarily incomplete but I have records of over 6,600 fires which coincided with his presence in the locality. A little calculation with my handy pocket calculator indicates that he very probably caused more than 14,000 fires during the 60 to 70 years of his wandering. Among these we must, I fear, include the second great fire of Toronto in 1904.

What does this all amount to, though, except for its interest as a juicy little scandal to enliven the meetings of this society? I would suggest, for one thing, that Nelson has to be seen as an economic factor of some importance in this province. The property damage of 14,000 fires was obviously enormous. It must, over the years, have had considerable impact on the province as capital was drained from useful investments to provide replacements for burned factories, &c. But it must also have had a considerable effect, in those days before government stimulation of the economy, in providing work for builders and thus diverting money from investments to the pockets of honest workmen. The effect on the insurance companies (*calls from audience: "No sales talk here tonight Ned." &c.*), which so often served as the channel for this flow of cash, must also have been highly stimulating. If they lost in the short run, they regained their money in the longer run by higher premiums, and had their utility to the community proved once again into the bargain. In none of this, however, will I go so far as to say that The Burner was a humanitarian or philanthropist. (*laughter from audience*) But a problem remains to be solved: How did he get away with it?

The answer to that, I think, also lies in my notes. He travelled incessantly, but it is to be noted that he seldom visited the same town or village twice within any period of ten or a dozen years. He never set a fire twice in the same community and he never, as far as I can tell, reappeared in any community where he had set a fire. Therefore, in a day of inadequate policing and poor communications between communities, he was relatively safe. A five year break in his record, however, when he disappears in Oshawa and reappears in Hamilton five years later, suggests that there may have been a prison term of which I am as yet unable to obtain a record.

I am glad to say that I have been able to uncover for you tonight a piece of the history of our town and province that needs to be incorporated, at least as a footnote, in the textbook histories. Why shouldn't Black Nelson be included? After all, he did almost as much harm as most premiers. (*laughter*) Though not as much perhaps as most premiers of the (censored) Party! (*roars of laughter*) It only remains for me to uncover the exact nature of his relations with the gambler Frederick Concert. When I consider that every other inmate of Concert's retirement home for Distressed Gentlefolks that I can trace was in some way a dependent of that unsavoury character or his wife, I doubt if he took Black Nelson the Burner in merely as a charity case. I rather think that in Fred I have had a predecessor in my research and in my estimate of Nelson' character. Perhaps I know now why Fred so seldom lost a card game! If I can get that proved, I will have a meaty address for some future meeting of our Society! And now I hand you over to the ladies, who have as usual I see prepared for us a bounteous repast!

Reppton History, vol. 12 (1960), pp. 16-25.

TRUE GRIT

Who remembers the billowing dust of the old gravel roads of Ontario? A speeding car or truck would streak along them like a meteorite and a solid screen of white dust would rise up like smoke of a forest fire. But time turns everything into the stuff of nostalgia. Today even the old gravel roads have their devotees. Rita and Carlsberg O'Lester, who spent their childhood holidays on just such roads as I have described, have written a finely illustrated book, which I am proud to introduce, *The Old Gravel Roads of Ontario*.

Readers who approach this subject with initial scepticism will be surprised to learn how large a section of the social history of this province turns on it. Three-quarters of the population of rural Ontario must have had permanent grit in its lungs in former days. The statistical connection established here between gravel roads and silicosis and tuberculosis will be debated for years. It is convincingly argued that the famous "T.B. houses", once so well known in rural Ontario – the houses where one member of the family after another died of T.B. – were situated in an unfortunate lie of the land where the wind enveloped them steadily in eddies and swirls of dust. Their inmates literally lived – and died – in the middle of a perpetual duststorm. It is a wonder the dust in people's food didn't grind their teeth flat, like the teeth of those Egyptian mummies who in life had fed on bread full of grit from the millstones. The Ontario dust was less abrasive than that, but it wore away enough of the protective covering of the teeth to ensure for country folk a rate of toothache that the authors calculate to be 50 per cent higher than that of city dwellers. The grit from the dusty roads of rural Ontario also habitually did for the machinery of local government what sand in the machinery normally does – it made the machinery malfunction noisily and occasionally come to a halt. Nothing was a more common cause of the overthrow of councils and the humiliation of reeves.

Yet amid these distresses and horrors, there is a brighter side to the subject. Rita and Carlsberg, in a series of dazzling photographs, show how the billowing and drifting dust on the surviving gravel roads makes wonderful effects with the sunlight, especially at dawn and at sunset. Those dust clouds cleared whole neighbourhoods of mosquitoes as effectively as the old mosquito smudges: the dust proved lethal in the delicate breathing mechanism of the mosquitoes. It was usually only when a period of continued wet weather kept the roads dustless for weeks that the mosquitoes began to come back in the hazy swarms the pioneers knew. Some scientists believe that the malaria which afflicted early Upper Canada was only eradicated when the gravel roads became effective enough to limit the numbers of mosquitoes.

The sadder side of human nature appears in the story of George Oliphantly, a country jeweller living near the village of Aranagusim, who painstakingly divided the most lacerating and needle-like particles of dust from the coarser remainder in order to use these deadly particles in poisoning his wife. He conjectured that Ontario road dust was the poison the authorities were least likely to suspect. He reckoned without his wife, who saw into the functions of his lab as clearly as himself, and into the workings of his diseased and tiny mind perhaps even a little more clearly, and he received life imprisonment. He spent the rest of his days breaking stones to make gravel for those dusty country roads.

Rita and Carlsberg have devoted 10 years to this project. Touring the hardbacked and gravelled roads of Ontario by car, bicycle and on foot, they have gained an unrivalled first hand knowledge of their subject. More than 1,500 interviews provide the generous human dimensions of this book. The same authors delighted readers a few years ago with their first book, the heavily illustrated *Old Swamps and Bogs of Ontario.*

INTRODUCTION BY R. ZOK TO R. AND C. O'LESTER,
The Old Gravel Roads of Ontario (1978).

THE PEPPER KING

Johnson Baker had been a merchant seaman and had seen the spice trade of the Far East. He had also been a lumberman in the Canadian woods and studied the flora there with the quick discerning eye that later roved with such precision among the columns of his account books in Baker's General Store. He conceived the idea that a wild pepper tree he had found growing in the mountains north of Montebello, Quebec, could be cultivated to yield a ground pepper good enough to compete successfully with the existing commercial brands. He planted 10 acres (later enlarged to 600 acres) of the wild pepper trees in the fields behind his general store. Nearby he established drying sheds, a grinding mill and warehouses from which the processed pepper was carried in sacks to its several destinations.

Baker's pepper was strong and cheap and gained so quickly in the markets that within a few years almost no other pepper was sold in Ontario or Quebec. There is a valuable essay by the late Harold Innis on the rise of Ontario as a pepper producer. He concludes with excitement that, "Seeing an opportunity to engage successfully global-metropolitan lines of communication in this trade, Baker leapt into dark waters commercially but coming ashore with his torch blazing he generally succeeded. But night was to follow, and the Great Depression, which threw Baker's pepper enterprises into the melting pot along with the global-metropolitan lines of communication he had vainly attempted to confront/supplant, arrived. The result was chaos."

As these much-quoted lines note, the Depression finished off poor Baker, who was forced to sell his interests and seek employment in Montreal where he died in 1942 in an explosion in a munitions factory. He is said to have been an early investor in the Montreal pizzerias. The Canadian pepper trade being at a standstill, his grove was cut and burned in 1946. The smoke, drifting over a portion of the county, killed off the field and garden crops and caused the Ilfitch Bank and Trust Co. no small sum in compensation.

M. RON, *A Pepper Kingdom in Ontario (1972)*.

EMENEUS BROWNSKILL

Among our eminent citizens in the years from the 1890s to the Second World War, no one was more influential in the affairs of the nation than Emeneus Brownskill, a professional writer of public school textbooks. He is said to have written more than 250 of the readers, spellers, arithmetics and other texts in standard use in the schools. What was unusual in the behaviour of Brownskill, a bachelor, was that he gradually shrank from public view and in the last 20 years or so of his career was a recluse.

When his big house was opened by the police the day after he died, it was found to be filled with books, many of them in the unopened packing crates in which they arrived, and old newspapers and magazines, none of more recent age than 30 years. There was a small amount of worn or damaged furniture and a quantity of dust that Mrs. Clifferfield, who got the job of cleaning up the place for the sale, said permanently injured her lungs and made her "like one of those gassed soldiers in the first war". The manuscripts and proofsheets of the last textbook on which Emeneus had worked were placed in the library of his old university. It was calculated by my brother, who is the town clerk, that Emeneus did five editions of his famous hygiene textbook in the years after the council began complaining that his house was a centre of rat-infestation for the whole town, and two of them after his septic tank collapsed and formed a pool in his back yard. Whenever I see one of my children's school textbooks now I think of the cattails round that pool.

I was talking to a bright young chap yesterday (I might as well admit he is my nephew) and he argues against a view that I have often heard expressed in town, that it must have made a dreadful impression on students to be taught from textbooks written by someone as out of touch as Emeneus. But my nephew thinks not, and says that Emeneus was like a sensitive thermometer as he measured the world getting worse, and that his withdrawal from it at last was a "creative act" (as my nephew calls it) and a step to promoting in students the instinct to duck as they see the old world coming their way.

C. LOWERS, *History of Orville (1974)*.

THE TRIBUTE

Since our last meeting, we have had the immeasurable sorrow of losing one of our most active members,

Mr. Mrs. Miss. Ms _____ twice _____ and _____ times _____ of this Society. Besides lending an enthusiastic hand to whatever work of fund raising, historical preservation or community education was in progress, _____ was an irrepressible historical researcher who contributed mightily over the past _____ years to the enlargement of our understanding of the past of our community. *(polite cheers)* _____ will be missed by all who knew him/her and looked forward to seeing his/her bright cheery smile at these meetings.

I ask this meeting of the Society to join me in expressing our warmest condolences to _____'s _____ and _____ .

The _____ and I have talked it over, and we are agreed that a fund must be started to provide a memorial prize, called the _____ Prize, to be awarded annually to _____ for _____ . The Society can contribute an initial sum of $_____, and it is expected that individual members of the Society will contribute a minimum of $_____ each. This fund will be a fitting and well-deserved tribute to _____ and will encourage the historical labours which he/she had so much at heart. I now wish to put this proposal before the Society for a vote. Can I have a motion? A seconder? The vote please, by raising hands. All for? _____ by _____ to _____ .

"Tips for Presidents" in SIDNEY WRIPS,
Running Your Own Historical Society (1979).

MICE

In those days the field mice, who ran about the sunlit fields all summer, used to pour into the houses in the fall to find abundant food and warmth for the winter. In vain did the wiry, athletic cats struggle to keep the mouse population down! Circulating through a hundred narrow channels where even the most shadow-thin cat could not follow, the mice were safe, except for those unwary or foolhardy representatives of their timid race who failed to take the necessary precautions as they ventured out by darkness into the living quarters of the house.

The problem will seem small to many people, but for over 20 years, in my work as a contractor specializing in the demolition and renovation of old houses, I have made an amusing hobby of taking elaborate notes on the wonderful networks used by mice in 19th-century houses. No two houses present quite the same data, but from over 600 village and country houses in the area of Centreville, Reealton and Clairseach Station, I am now prepared to generalize on the locations of mouse passages in these old houses. The famous Bishop of Bingen in his Mouse Tower on the Rhine apparently didn't know how it was done – but I do. For anyone who wishes to check my conclusions from the original data, I have kept careful notes well supplemented by photographs. In due time I will place these in the Ontario Archives or the University of Waterloo Library. Though fortune has been good to me and I have grown to be (I believe in being frank) one of the richest citizens of the area, I confess that I could have been richer still if I had turned my attention to the most financially rewarding part of my profession, namely developing new housing. But such has been my love for my research that I have preferred to stay with those old houses where I found my dear mouse lore.

From the introduction to F. Catagusluch's sumptuously illustrated coffee table book, *Mouse Channels in Old Houses (1977)*.

THE McCOLLS,
A REVOLUTIONARY FAMILY

Our family has distinguished itself in Canada from early times by a particular talent for inventing and collecting taxes. The first of our family to arrive here was enterprising Joshua McColl, who joined the North West Company as a mere boy in 1800. His proposal by which the Company would tax the Indians within its trading area was rejected on the grounds of his youth. But his next proposal, by which the faltering company would buy and farm the taxes of Montreal, was so well received by his colleagues that only the outbreak of riots and arson in the city at the end of 1818 prevented its implementation. About this time he married Miss Celine De Courcey, whose grandfather had served the French regime in Quebec as a tax adviser. His emergency scheme to tax the French soldiers' wages is said to have carried the government through a bad patch in 1758 but unfortunately to have caused discontent that hastened the fall of Quebec the following year.

Joshua had five sons and four daughters. Over the following decades we find his sons and daughters diligently scouring Upper Canada for local taxes. It cannot be doubted that this was a discouraging period in the history of the McColls. Taxes were so low that they barely met the expenses of collection.

To illustrate the humble, hardworking life of these sons and daughters we have a typical incident from the diary of Frederick McColl. One afternoon in October 1850, he records, he travelled for eight miles in pelting rain over bog-like country roads in a hired hay cart which he had to pry out of the clay with fence rails on over 20 occasions. The aim of the journey was to collect two shillings in back taxes from a blacksmith who was so rich that he floored his parlour in American marble. The rich blacksmith paid Frederick one shilling, with threats to set his mastiff on the unhappy lad if he called for the second shilling before the shantymen came home in the spring.

Governments, meanwhile, were deaf to the proposals which Joshua with such foresight, produced for a modernized and productive taxation system for the province. Though his talents were little valued and underused at home, he developed a reputation abroad. His correspondence with the British reformer Jeremy Bentham on the rationalization of taxation systems has been published. In the same period the Sultan of Turkey adopted a plan which Joshua presented for a tax on surplus females and rewarded him with an ostrich egg filled with solid gold. It is said that by some oriental art the shell was so replaced on the gold that not even the most cunning eye could detect a break in it. His friend William Lyon Mackenzie said that not even the weight could convince him that there was gold in an egg so evidently unbroken. But when the shell was chipped off before a large assembly at the legislative building in York, the doubts of Mackenzie and all others were laid to rest. Joshua McColl also considerably interested Czar Nicholas I in a scheme for a special tax on the families of political prisoners but although he spent much time on the scheme and even travelled once to Russia to consult with imperial officials, it is clear that he was never paid for his labours. On whether or not the scheme was adopted, historians must have the final say, but Lenin's recommendation in his *Emergency Address* of 1922 that *"M. McColl's ingenious and socially constructive scheme be adopted at once"* seems to imply that up to then it had not been in use consistently if at all.

Our ancestor Joshua's plans for a revision of the Canadian tax system were summed up in a little book called *Whose Money? The People's? The Public's!!!*, to which William Lyon Mackenzie wrote a preface. It is to be feared that the book was so completely misunderstood everywhere that it immediately became the most unpopular book ever to have been published in the province. Joshua used to lament in his old age that if the Tories had not so relentlessly circulated copies of it to every country store and backwoods settlement, and in short to every bestial nook and cranny of ignorance and prejudice in the country, Mackenzie's rebellion would have won enough support to have enabled him to turn Upper Canada into an American state. Joshua was in exile in the American South for some years after the failure of the rebellion. His pamphlet showing that slavery as practised in the United States was regressive because it was inconsistent with rationalized systems of universal taxation was long a revered work in abolitionist circles. However, his life was no longer safe anywhere the power of slavery extended, and it was doubtless for this reason that he returned in 1861 to the province of Upper Canada (now Canada West) which he always called the most ignorant in taxation matters in the whole world.

He spent the remaining years of his life at the very centre of the brilliant little intellectual circle then flourishing in Toronto and died in 1868, being, in the prophetic words of his American friend Horace Greeley, still 33 years short of the century to which he belonged. Karl Marx, who had met him in Toronto in 1865 (EDITOR'S NOTE: *See pp. 42-43*) wrote to Engels that,

"The late Mr. KcKoll in his backwoods grasped what nobody else but ourselves has done, that the capitalist state's renunciation of its taxation powers must itself in turn be renounced if the capitalist state is to continue. It cannot be that the capitalist state itself will recognize its error, resume its abandoned taxing powers and strengthen itself with bands of steel that could make it unassailable for centuries to come. That such cannot happen, we know on the grounds that the victory of the proletariat must come before so great a reorientation of capitalism itself, theoretically feasible though it is in itself, can be established. It was only the latter point that Mr. McKoll did not perfectly understand."

Three of his grandsons, feeling that their particular talents would have no scope in the government employment of the day, directed themselves to growing rich in their law practices in Toronto. In their spare time they peppered successive federal and provincial premiers (most of whom were personal friends) with well-prepared briefs recommending a more advanced and comprehensive system of taxation for Canada, as first worked out by their grandfather and since further refined by themselves and other members of the family. It can hardly be doubted that the influence of these briefs, so persistently held up to the attention of statesmen for so many years, and backed as they were by the personal charm of the three brothers, gradually shifted official opinion in Canada from the 19th-century concept of low taxation (or *"no taxation"*, as Joshua always contemptuously called it) to the 20th-century system of the modern state taxing as freely as its social needs demand.

At this point we must pause to honour one of the almost unknown makers of modern Canada. Miss Alicia McColl, a first cousin of the three lawyers, lived in retirement on a private income in Kingston, Ontario. Consistent ill health made her, like Charles Darwin and Elizabeth Barrett

Browning, one of the great sofa-bound intellectuals of the Victorian age. But in her incessant studies, pursuing lines of thought that led her whole generations beyond those of her contemporaries, she became a thinker whose unpublished papers were studied eagerly by Keynes and a woman who, in the words of one of her modern admirers, *"created single handedly, in provincial isolation, out of her own unaided brain, the philosophy and technique of taxation as they exist in the modern superstates"*. It is not hard to guess that many of the ideas which her cousins so diligently and successfully propagated among the men of power came in the first instance from her darkened study. Always shy of the public gaze, she published nothing. Barely 20 people are said to have attended her funeral in Kingston where she died in 1928 at the age of 91.

It is sad to report that in the critical period in which big taxation came into being in Canada, that is, from about 1914 to 1945, our family's attention seems to have wandered elsewhere. The McColls produced lawyers, doctors, professors of literature, millionaire businessmen and a few of the inevitable black sheep that any large talented family produces, but not one philosopher of taxation or even one practicing tax man. In our family, talent skipped a generation. But the teachings of Joshua McColl, his three lawyer grandsons and Miss Alicia were percolating through the whole structure of Canadian society and government. Their hour finally came and today they influence Canadians in every hour of our lives.

I was delighted to confirm at the family reunion last year in Ottawa how many McColls of the present generation are professionally involved in taxation. My husband and I counted civil servants (some of the highest rank), tax lawyers, accountants, bankers, business consultants, computer technologists and professors – and still like the kings in Macbeth, our kindred came on in endless procession.

SUSAN ALICIA MCCOLL-STOPFORD, *The McColls (1979)*.

OLD CHARACTERS

A SCHOOLMASTER

In the old days we had many teachers who were abject human wrecks, driven by a craving for drink into the lower depths of poverty and thence (always downward) into the ranks of rural schoolmasters. But we also had men of monumental character , possessing sometimes degrees from foreign universities, always inculcating, frequently with a good cedar whip taken from the abundant cedar swamps, the supreme utility of Greek, Latin, French, algebra, Euclid, trigonometry, ethics, rhetoric, natural history and political economy. Among such, none was more a giant in his day, or remembered with more awe after,

> "His sun had set
> And sorrowing yet
> His trooping mourners
> Homeward trekt"

than Adam Smith Bairdeen, a boyhood friend and lifelong correspondent of Thomas Carlyle, and supposed on good grounds to be the *"Canadian Schoolmaster"* addressed with the words *"Flail on Brave Schoolmaster, till you see the Flash of the White of the Bone"*, in the opening lines of Carlyle's essay, *The Schoolmaster as King in His Own Domain.* When Bairdeen died all his letters from Carlyle were burned by the reeve, who said he didn't want bookishness further encouraged in the township.

M. MARTIN, *Old Days Remembered (1933).*

THEIR WORK WAS UNDERGROUND

From about Confederation till the opening years of this century, a grisly but profitable trade of rural Ontario was robbing graves to supply cadavers to medical students. In one case, well known to my grandfather, a medical student who began to work his way through college by robbing graves and selling the occupants to his more affluent fellow students found his business so easy and profitable that he abandoned the pursuit of medicine and went into grave robbing full time. His son later became a distinguished bone surgeon. It is said that as a token of especial esteem his father presented him on his day of graduation with the skeleton of a well-known multimillionaire benefactor of the university in which he had studied.

But in no town other than our own, so far as my knowledge extends, was the whole prosperity of the town based on grave robbing. The origins of this lay in the enterprise of Ludovicus Rasp, a native of New Brunswick, who inherited a farm in this district from his uncle. The farm did not pay and Lud, who had a lifelong aversion to anything that did not pay, went into the grave robbing business to make ends meet. He first robbed the local cemeteries then, hiring labourers and teams of swift horses, he organized the trade further afield. His exact attention to railway timetables ensured a smooth flow of the cadavers to the medical schools in Toronto, Kingston, Montreal, Buffalo and New York. Building up a cash reserve in this manner, he used it to found a small shoe factory on his farm. This is today of course the parent plant of the famous Rasp Shoe Co. The farm has long since disappeared (though I can remember the orchard) beneath the subdivisions of workers' houses necessitated by the plant.

Lud gradually gave up grave robbing as the plant absorbed more and more of his attention but one incident from the history of the company has been deservedly told and retold by the oldtimers who used to gather in the staff cafeteria or Rasp's General Store or Miss Rasp's Cafe. It seems that about 1910 a financial panic in the shoe industry suddenly put Lud into the rare position of being unable to meet his payroll. It was his boast that he had never failed an employee or a creditor yet and he was determined that this would not become the first time. That night he organized his sons and a posse of his most trusted employees and, with shovels and company wagons, they set off about midnight to all points of the compass. Within a few days enough money had come back from Montreal, Toronto and other points to meet the upcoming payroll for the next month.

This stout old entrepreneur was returned without opposition as our MP from 1922 to 1929. His ambition was to be a Senator, but it is said he was considered ineligible for that exclusive house on the grounds that a man who was believed to have lifted the body of more than one Senator was unworthy to sit there. He died in 1932 and is commemorated by a splendid marble tomb in his old New Brunswick village. By his own directions his body was cremated and the ashes scattered in the River Crepton where the waste from his factory furnaces was usually deposited. How many young men of today, repulsed by the loan companies but with a vision of commercial empire, would show the enterprise of this successful Maritimer?

R. PRACHT, *Where Rasp Shoes Began (1946)*.

Jamie was the poet of our town. It is sad to report that this gifted man had to earn his living as a body-snatcher. So delicate was his ear that it is said he could judge the exact worth of a coffin, and from that the probable wealth of the family, by the tone of the first *"ting"* (as it was called in the grave robbing trade) as his shovel hit the pine.

71

THEIR WORK WAS UNDERGROUND

His early poems dwell on the effects of moonlight on the shifting leaves of the Lombardy poplars, on the long velvety shadows that these tall graceful trees draped across the fields of white tombstones, on the rich night smell of wet earth, on the distant howling of dogs as the heavy clods of earth were thrown out of the reopened graves, and on the mist and the rain that sometimes drove like a shovelpoint down from the hills, suddenly enveloping the men in darkness in the midst of their work. In his later years he turned to more sober images of pale puffed faces, fallen leaves, loose grave-earth, ankle-deep about the diggers' boots, moonlit snowlike fields of fire about the tombstones and the dark lanterns that he represented so feelingly as symbols of Hope and Insight alternating with Despair and Utter Darkness.

His place among the *"Confederation Poets"*, as they are called, is secure. He has been the subject of several serious scholarly enquiries in recent years. A thesis on his works is likely to be published soon by our leading university press. Its projected title is *The Yorick Game*. But it has long been believed in our area that by far the best of his poems have been destroyed, possibly by his niece and executrix, who thought them damaging to her millinery business. In my youth, oldtimers could still recite whole stanzas that seemed better to my youthful ear (sharper in these matters, I am sorry to say, than my more mature ear, but for two-thirds of our life we are declining) than anything of his that ever appeared in print. Archibald Lampman, who knew many of the unpublished poems by heart, is said to have declared that Jamie had outdistanced him and all the other Canadian poets of their generation by a shankbone. There was talent in the literary men of Jamie's generation that I do not think is found among their successors today.

F. ZWICKERS, *Personages of Ipton Township (1950)*.

Summary of Research. For this project more than 150,000 file cards of data were collected. These were collated by a team of three clerical workers chosen for their familiarity with computer terminology and statistical methods. The work was supported by a grant of $50,000 from the Social Studies Research Council (SSRC). One of the conclusions reached was that in the years 1870 to 1890, in the block of six counties studied, farm incomes were on the average consistently lower than farm expenditures. Such sources as casual labour in lumbercamps and nearby cities was easily shown to have filled up 65 per cent of the gap. But how the remainder of the gap was filled remained for long a mystery to the researchers. It was only when they came to follow up a clue provided by Mr. Eldred McZost, the oldest citizen of Nooshton, that they discovered that almost every farm home in these years drew an occasional income from grave robbing. On calculation, this income was found to be large enough to fill the gap and thus bring the total income and total expenditures of the six county block into balance with each other. It is suggested that the conclusions that have been established for this limited area may also apply with equal force to the whole of the province. It is also suggested that a satisfactorily funded research unit should be set up to investigate this possibility. It is further calculated (see Appendix V) that an annual grant of $50,000 from the SSRC in each of five years should be sufficient to see this project to completion.

S. FREETON, *"Farm Incomes and Expenditures in the Portach District",*
report, 1978.

R. CORNFOLL AND C. RUDOLF

Rudolf Cornfoll was schoolmaster of our town from 1853 to 1875. If the typical schoolteacher of today is Miss Nice, the typical schoolteacher of that era was Mr. Ugly. And although it is among the Mr. Uglies we must certainly place Rudolf Cornfoll, it must also be admitted that he was a man of strong genius who developed several notions peculiar to himself and clung to them with incredible tenacity.

He persuaded himself that the date of building the Canadian railway system had been placed far too late by Canadian historians and that the various military manoeuvres of the War of 1812, which have been so baffling to historians, could only be made intelligible by the assumption that a full-fledged Canadian passenger and freight service was already running between Montreal and Toronto in those years. Surprisingly, a distinguished Royal Military University historian who examined Rudolf's notes on this subject during Centennial Year has conceded that, although he remains totally unconvinced that any Canadian railway was operating between 1812 and 1814, innumerable difficulties and inconsistencies in the accepted narrative of the war can only be explained by the hypothesis that this railway system *was* in existence.

While in his periodic black fits of drunkenness (for he was a very hard, a very vicious and a most explosive-tempered drinker) Rudolf used to assert that in 1813 his grandfather and his six stout sons, armed only with pitchforks, had stopped a whole trainload of Yankee soldiers at Port Hope Station on the Montreal-Toronto line. They disarmed the soldiers, turned them out of the train and imprisoned them, with farmers as guards, in six local Orange Halls.[1] Having repeated this assertion several times in his famous foghorn voice, he would challenge anyone to contradict him. His fellow roisterers, well remembering the Herculean strength of his great whipping arm, would hasten to assert that they did not have a doubt in the world about his story.

Another of his beliefs was that medicine in Canada could not possibly advance by importation of remedies which were invariably contrary to the air and natural constitution of the country, but that a new and distinct set of Canadian medicines would need to be worked out from the herbs which grew in abundance in the Canadian fields and forests. To this end, he applied for many years a small income which he made on the side by money-lending (often to his students, and more often to their parents) to the employment of a variety of Indian, German, French Canadian, and other herb doctors, whose knowledge, collections and theories were put to the test in his lab where he compiled his conclusions in a Latin manuscript. Unhappily, no publisher in Canada in the 1870s would touch a Latin manuscript, with the result that he had to ship it to Germany to be printed. There it was lost in a fire in a print shop in Bremen set by French saboteurs revenging the annexation of Alsace-Lorraine. According to a variant of this story the manuscript was saved from the flames by a learned firefighter[2] and became the source of a number of well-received German doctoral theses over the next 20 years.

Surprisingly for a man so well known for his furious Toryism in his mature years, Rudolf had once been a boon companion of William Lyon Mackenzie. But from the early '70s onwards he was fond of repeating, in a voice of great earnestness that moved everyone who heard it, a prediction of a Gypsy woman he had employed in his herb gatherings that William Lyon Mackenzie would have a grandson who would turn into an old woman and would be the absolute ruin of his nation. He is also said to have predicted, on his own account, the two World Wars and the destruction of Kingston, Ontario by either a tsunami or a student insurrection in 1995.[3] In the hot August of 1875, one day after the arsonist Liddfield boys (sons of old "Arson" Liddfield, the tanner) burned down the dog pound, Rudolf Cornfoll abruptly left town and no local enquiries ever succeeded in tracing him again. Enquiries I made in preparing this study proved equally unavailing.

R. SCHULER, *Schoolmasters of Yore (1980)*.

Notes

[1] I am informed by my friend Mr. Durchas Pfald, of Port Hope, that one of the early unsolved mysteries of that town is the appearance, packed in six Orange Halls, of several hundred American infantrymen in 1813. Some of them were persuaded to marry local girls and settle as farmers in the wild country back of the town. The rest of them were put to work clearing farms for the leading local citizens or were imprisoned under the direction of a mysterious Mr. Samuel Divers in what must have been one of the world's earliest barbed wire prison camps. They managed, one by one and in groups, to escape and drift back as vagrants to their homes in the United States. By 1816 the camp was empty.

76

[2]Conceivably Karl Marx's brother Alfred, who was a firefighter in Bremen and the source of much of his brother's knowledge of German working class life. In 1890 he was prosecuted for running a trade in spurious doctoral theses.
See Tom McColbert, *A Proletarian Marx (1968).*

[3]Against my advice, my friend Mr.Bearr McVol, of Werkton, near Prescott, is preparing a book on the Ontario prophets and has found much rich ore. The prophecies of Norman Asdair of Brockville were put into verse by Archibald Lampman but have never been made public for copyright reasons. The Larchwood Commune set up near Gananoque in the 1960s was interested in prophecies. It was noted that while its prophecies remained remarkably accurate for events up till about the early 1970s, for a later period they were invariably wrong. We must dismiss as a modern fiction or at least as most improbable a prophecy said to have been spoken by Robert Gourlay at a public meeting at Prescott in 1820,

"That in the year 1999 the whole colony would be visited regularly by great travellers from Japan, who would travel in long carriages called buses and would paint pictures of the inhabitants with a device called a camera. And that the inhabitants would beat their hands on the sides of the buses and cry 'baksheesh', 'baksheesh', and 'tips', 'tips'."

In September 1875 there arrived in our flourishing backwoods village of McGatroyd the heavily-bearded and almost cubical figure of Cornfoll Rudolf, who quickly established a prosperous business as doctor, lawyer, librarian, general merchant, ironmonger and architect. Although of a volcanic temper when aroused by drink, (he was unfortunately too often drunk) such was his standing in the town, and such the sweetness and charm of his conversation on innumerable topics when he was sober and happy, that he was mayor of McGatroyd for the first six years after its incorporation as a town. Perhaps the most learned man ever to reside in our town he corresponded with Matthew Arnold, Walt Whitman and Henry Adams; his letters from them are still in the Carnegie Library on Cornfoll Rudolf Street. He is believed to have launched Stephen Leacock's literary career by editing *Literary Lapses* from the half dozen unfinished novels Leacock brought to his door one day in 1906.

He died in 1914, one week after the outbreak of war, being then about 95 years old. His death is supposed to have been hastened by public revulsion against his suggestion that Canada should declare war on Great Britain. He left no publications under his own name but a celebrated temperance pamphlet, which was given away in scores of millions of copies in the United States, is said to have been from his hand. He would never acknowledge it, probably because although he defended the temperance cause at all times with crushing logic, he was totally unable to control his own drinking.

Of his life before he came to McGatroyd he was resolute in never speaking, and although I have done much research into the question while preparing this book I am as ignorant about it as when I began. I feel I must agree with several townsfolk I have discussed him with that a life so well concealed was probably not very creditable. A female tramp claiming to be his granddaughter is said to have obtained a free meal at Wally's cafe in 1935 before disappearing into the night, but because of ill health I have been unable to follow up this story.

MYRTLE MORE, *McGatroyd (1981)*.

DISCOVERIES

TO THE EDITOR, SIR: My uncle was one of that quiet generation of late 19th-century civil servants in Ottawa whose homes were but a few blocks from their tranquil offices and who often kept a cow or two in their back yards, as a hobby and for milk, and who had abundant leisure to become learned in all manner of subjects. In the case of my uncle the subject was Indians and he compiled, over the years, an impressive collection of data to prove that Parliament Hill, about the mid-17th century, had been the location of a great wooden castle built by a tribe of Indians hitherto unknown to investigators.

These Indians, according to his research, had developed their own system of mummifying their dead, not unlike that of the Egyptians, and their own system of writing in hieroglyphics on a papyrus-type paper. A race of deer-hunters, they used the castle primarily as a storehouse for their mummies and their documents. It was raided and burned by marauding fur traders about 1690. The Indians retreated to the American far west, where traces of their devotion to paperwork are reported by explorers and soldiers as late as 1905. The last member of the tribe served as a Quartermaster Embalmer in the American Army in the Great War. In private life, he was the principal author of the well-known Dotwell System of keeping undertakers' accounts. Earlier, when the American Civil War was raging, the American government consulted the remnants of the tribe in connection with the art of embalming, which (as is well known) the American government was reviving to enable the burial at home of the dead soldiers.

I naturally never took these doctrines of my uncle's very seriously, regarding them as an example of those extravagances of thought that often afflict elderly collectors who have become too withdrawn to allow their ideas to be refined by the free give and take of debate with other scholars. But some evidence has recently come to light to make me look more tolerantly on this good old gentleman and his speculations. The workmen who last week sank deep trenches around the southeast corner of the Parliament Buildings have uncovered a series of massive pine tree trunks driven deep into bore holes in the rock and scored on the sides in a manner reminiscent of the early Irish Ogham writing. The tops of these trunks show charring. They cannot have been a part of the structure of the present or the first Parliament Buildings on this site, as a layer of undisturbed leaf mould of many years' accumulation stood above them before excavation. Can my uncle's theories have been correct? I await the opinions of your readers on this, and I wish the present government would appoint some competent archaeologist to investigate the question searchingly.

I am your obt. servt., J. J. Milsom.

Ottawa Tribune, 22 July 1937. Reprinted in K. RENTZ, *Before Ottawa (1968).*

WEEDS IN HISTORY

Some kinds of people are almost always pleasant. Among such I would include, on the basis of my own experience, military and naval historians, the people who attend dog and cat shows and local historians. But in this last group I must admit that I have been caused much grief by one or two exceptions.

In our neighbourhood few families have maintained a higher reputation for a longer time than the Belterns. Only a few of my readers will remember the name of Angus Beltern. But Angus was a power in his day, as a lawyer and a Liberal Party organizer in his district, as one of the prolific early contributors to *Ontario History* and as a researcher in local history who was looked up to by all who worked in that fascinating but often difficult field. Angus' discovery that a party of U.E. Loyalists had ascended the St. Lawrence River as early as 1780 and established a village on the present site of Kitchener was one of the historical breakthroughs of his day and, although never committed to print by himself, was quickly adopted, usually without giving credit to him, by a multitude of other writers.

But I do not know how it was that Angus grew more and more bitter as the years passed. His friends began to withdraw from him and he settled down to a project of research that I could never regard as anything but a needless piece of malignancy, namely an enquiry into the names and careers of those unfortunates who introduced the principal noxious weeds into Ontario – the burdock, Scotch thistle, ragweed, dandelion and so forth.

79

He worked very hard for many years and compiled a very large manuscript. I remember that the section on the burdock was about 20 pages long. It briskly outlined the history of this noxious weed in the Old World and showed with some eloquence what a curse it has been in the New. It proved with many references to sources that a certain – of –, (I charitably suppress all names) who was a prominent farmer and the uncle of one of our country's few philanthropists, deliberately imported the burdock seeds and sowed them on the property of a neighbouring widow with whom he and his sons had had a scandalous relationship. Not frustrated love but a refusal on the part of the widow to sell her property to him for a token sum and become the manageress of a boarding house he had obtained by forging a will was his motive for this disgraceful crime. Nor in leafing through Angus' manuscript was this the only time I came upon a family name that was a household word to Canadians. It isn't a very harmful weed perhaps, but do you know which of our most distinguished Canadian writers had an ancestor who introduced the mullein to Canada?

When Angus died his widow put the manuscript in my hands to publish or destroy as I saw best,

I did not hesitate for a moment to commit it in her presence to the flames in the furnace of the old milk plant. Only once since then have I indiscreetly communicated any of the information I found in its pages. When Mr. William Lyon Mackenzie King visited this town in 1926 I was assigned to entertain him, which was not a very easy task I am afraid, for he was the most shy and retiring man I have ever met. For lack of a better topic common to the both of us, I began to speak of Angus, whom he had known well. From there I went on to discuss Angus' book on the noxious weeds and – I confess this with shame – I entertained the great man with several of the most scandalous anecdotes in the book, neither omitting the names nor sparing anyone's reputation. He chuckled a great deal, with an odd little silvery sound, and showed his two rows of very even little teeth, like the tiny kernels of those baby ears of corn that women pickle. He seemed to take particular pleasure in the information about the prominent Manitoba political family of –, and when I had, as I thought, finished my disgraceful tattling, he reeled off a whole list of prominent persons to me, asking which ones were represented in any way (and a few were) in the manuscript. I did not know at this time that he kept a diary. I have been reading about this diary in the newspapers and it troubles me that he may well have copied out into the diary some of the information I had been so anxious to suppress. If so, some of Angus' malicious discoveries may be made known to the world yet. I am privileged to know that one of the most irritating American television talk show personalities of our time is the direct descendant of an old Canadian lady believed by her neighbours to be an abortionist and a witch, and who tried to sow a poisonous Bengali mushroom in her neighbour's garden.

C. OSP, *An Old Man Remembers (1972)*.

THE AGE OF
MACDONALD AND LAURIER

THE SIR JOHN A. MACDONALD
MYSTERY SOLVED

About halfway between Guelph and Silvern, where the road runs across a little iron bridge, the observant traveller can still spot among the sand hills of Mr. Green's sheep pasture the half-buried foundations of a considerable number of houses. This is all that remains of one of the earliest villages of Ontario and the birthplace of Sir John A. Macdonald. About the year 1780, before the grant of the Grand River lands was made to Joseph Brant, a former Boston merchant called Douglas O'Hara, who had been driven out of the Colony of Massachusetts for his unyielding loyalty to the Crown, ascended the Grand River with a flotilla of small boats and rafts and a party of 20 followers and, at the spot I have just described, founded a village which he called Loyalty.

The question of which side burned the flourishing textile manufacturing town of Loyalty to the ground in the War of 1812 is one to which I shall return later in this sketch. Some of the villagers claimed compensation and were granted new freeholds in the towns of Waterloo and Berlin and Loyalty, henceforth, was *"one with Ninevah and Tyre"*.

A watercolour of the town made by Mrs. Simcoe about 1795, in the most highly-coloured style of her much admired El Greco period, shows a short row of five-storey frame tenement buildings on either side of the main street (Loyal Bay Colony Street) and a maze of cabins amid which, here and there, (for some reason, O'Hara liked his factories tall rather than wide) a factory building of squared logs stood up like a square silo. At the northeast corner of the town, surrounded by a large green field, was Loyalty House, the log home of Douglas O'Hara, a pitiably reduced imitation of the brick mansion he had owned at Watertown, near Boston.

The French traveller and political philosopher, the Duc de Crie-Vilain, who visited Upper Canada in the late 1790s in search of social conditions close to those under which the Social Contract was signed, has left a description of the town. In this delightful manuscript we learn that O'Hara had imposed a decimal system of time on the town by which the day was divided into 10 hours, five being hours of darkness and five hours of daylight. The operatives in the mills worked during the five hours of daylight but were paid the low winter rate in all seasons, though under O'Hara's decimal system the summer hours were of course much longer. It was one of O'Hara's strictest rules that no artificial light of any kind should ever be used in the town. Crie-Vilain described O'Hara as a common oppressor of the labourers and farmers of his settlement, *"plus mal que*

Robespierre". He added that like our father Jacob, he had two wives, and clove to one while he hated the other. He was truly married to both of them, the duke reported with quiet irony, for O'Hara had laid down all the rules for marriages in his town and had performed both marriage services himself.

I began many years ago to reconstruct the history of this colony so out of keeping, in many ways, with the Upper Canadian civilization growing around it. It was not, however, till I had retired from the Accounting Department of Nimh Chemical Extraction that I was able to direct myself full time to my hobby. I went to England and spent some months studying O'Hara's papers in the Public Record Office. I was especially interested at this stage in disentangling the genealogy of his many descendants. One of them was Macken O'Hara, the treasurer of J. - F. Papineau. This young man with a head for figures appeared to have arranged the whole financing of Papineau's rebellion through business sources in Cornwall, Ontario who were hoping to terrify the British government into annexing Montreal to Upper Canada. Another descendant was the celebrated American poisoner Mrs. Oliver who, after leaving a 10-year trail of death and terror through the boarding houses of the Mississippi Valley and the slave states, received a pardon from President Grant for her espionage services and spent her last years as an appointments secretary in the White House. But a connection of deeper interest to Canadians than either of these began to come to light. I had known, of course, of an old legend in the Loyalty neighbourhood, that it was the birthplace of our first Prime Minister. But now I found the entry for the birth of O'Hara's seventh son, which read,

"VII. John A. Macdonald, born 11 Jan. 1814, to Douglas O'Hara, himself a Seventh Son, and his wife Carmilla Zabrillo, daughter of a refugee physician from Mantua."

This son, like all the children born to the wife O'Hara hated, had been given a fictitious surname chosen in alphabetical order.

But if this was our first Prime Minister, how did he come to be supplied with a new set of parents from Scotland and an apparent place of birth in that country? To piece together the answer to this story took many more months of research in old newspapers, family records and government documents.

The key was the mysterious destruction of the town in May 1814. In the course of my research I saw clearly that the destruction was carried out not by the British or the American forces in the War of 1812, but by the townspeople themselves, who rose up in rage against the oppression of O'Hara and his clique. They burned the hated factories in which they had been no better than slaves and the tenements and log houses which they feared would, if left standing, provide an excuse one day for rebuilding the factories. The enraged townspeople blocked up all the wells with stones, smashed down all fences, drove the cattle and fowl into the wilderness and trooped off in the direction of York, alleging themselves to be war refugees. O'Hara's two wives fled to Detroit, from where they wrote several letters to their old friend Laura Secord (a frequent guest at Loyalty House) betraying American military secrets which that energetic lady lost no time in conveying to the British authorities. Later they ran a boarding house in Portsmouth, England where their interest in naval data caused much disquiet in the Admiralty. They were persuaded, in return for a large sum of money, to transfer their boarding house business to an inland village in County Galway, Ireland and there their trail ends. We may fear that O'Hara's trail ended at the bottom of one of those blocked up wells that the fleeing occupants of his town left behind them. A job, perhaps, for the archaeologist.

Since most of O'Hara's children reappear among the claimants who were resettled by the British government at Waterloo and Berlin, we may suppose that they were carried away in the original flow of refugees to York. (Some of the German families of Kitchener-Waterloo, incidentally, derive their German surnames from the fictitious names given by O'Hara to the sons of his hated wife Carmilla, the mother of our first Prime Minister). Among the fugitives from Loyalty must have been a baby, the young John A., who would have been marked out among these superstitious people as an especial personage, not because he was the son of the dominating and magnetic tyrant O'Hara, but because he was *the seventh son of a seventh son*. There is no record that he was ever granted lands in the Waterloo-Berlin area. He next appears as an "orphan" being kept by the O'Hara widows in their boarding house at Portsmouth. In 1820, exactly the same time that these ladies migrated to Galway, the young John A. Macdonald set out by ship from Glasgow to Canada under the guise of being the son of a Mr. and Mrs. Hugh Macdonald. Who this Mr. and Mrs. Macdonald were we need not enquire very deeply, but they were probably a M. and Mme. Lefland, refugees from the French Revolution who had lived for some years in Aberdeen. But in the years preceding the breakup of the O'Haras' Portsmouth boarding house had been employed there as cook and gardener.

From this point onwards the life of the future Sir John A. Macdonald is one of the best documented in Canadian history. Yet what I have outlined about his true origins will certainly answer a few questions about his career which have continued to baffle even his most diligent researchers. Why in 1882 did he place a marble plaque in Mantua in honour of an emigre Italian revolutionary and physician, Dr. Zabrillo? (The plaque was removed in 1928 during Mussolini's campaign against incorrect Latin inscriptions.) Why in 1886 did Macdonald order from the Dublin monumental sculptor, James Pearse, (father of the Irish martyr of 1916, Patrick Pearse or MacPiarais two marble tombs for an unnamed County Galway cemetery? But most of all, what I have outlined explains why Macdonald, ordinarily the most practical of visionaries, pushed for so many years in his private correspondence with the British government the project of establishing a decimal system of time exactly like that reported to have been used by his father Douglas O'Hara.

C. CRAIGS, *Loyalty (1962)*.

THE NECKLACE OF FIRE

In the old days in the province there were many festivals that are now forgotten. In the strip of country that extends from Niagara Falls along the lake to Windsor, for example, there was the autumn festival of fire which took place on a date in October established every year by astrologers in Toronto. In those days smaller towns normally did not have astrologers. On the night appointed the logs and branches that had been piled up during the summer were all set aflame at the same time. The resulting curve of fire along the lake shore was known as the Queen's Necklace – a name sometimes interpreted as a tribute to Queen Victoria and sometimes as a clue to the pagan origins of the festival. There was not lacking a darker interpretation, which held that at some point along this line of fire a maiden had to be sacrificed in the flames and that hers was the "necklace of fire". It was said that the old people believed that if the sacrifice failed to take place for even one year, Lake Erie would flow over the land and not cease its advance till the time for the next sacrifice came round. Sir Philemon Jones, the oriental philologist, who travelled through the province in 1864 to visit his brother, a trapper and hermit at Rat Portage, is said to have investigated the festival and to have been struck by its similarity to ceremonies he had observed on the Malabar coast of India. It is said that Egerton Ryerson was especially anxious to place primary schools and secondary schools in precisely those areas where devotion to the necklace of fire festival was strongest, with a view to breaking it up by the progress of knowledge. When my brother was a young man he had an insatiable craving for drink, which he later mastered to become a perfect teetotaler and one of the wealthiest and most influential citizens in his part of the province. But while he was in this juvenile state of weakness, grovelling in his bondage, one of his boon drinking companions, in a fit of the recklessness and relaxation of all restraints which drink brings upon its devotees, told him, as a secret upon which his life depended, that the last human sacrifice had occurred in 1888. The next sacrifice, intended for 1889, was prevented by the appearance of Sir John A. Macdonald, who so jollied and scolded the would-be participants in this dark deed that they retreated to their homes leaving the maiden unharmed. She was subsequently enrolled in a Toronto home for training domestics and kept a very respectable lodging house in Ottawa for many years and had MPs of the highest rank among her boarders. That year the lake did not advance to cover the land and the old superstition was discredited forever. Sir John seems to have exacted a pledge from the people that if the floods did not occur they would abandon not only their detestable practice of human sacrifice but the entire festival, which even if continued as a purely innocent amusement carried too much temptation for weaker and more superstitious minds. I see from the *Globe* that there are now dangerous proposals to revive it in a few localities as a good old pioneer custom which boys might be content to regard as a harmless substitute for Hallowe'en.

J. M'RESTON, *West of Toronto (1939)*.

BURIED DEEPLY

Forty-seven years are surely enough! That is the time I have spent in prison for a crime I did not commit. What was this crime you will ask? I was a simple barber in the small town of Habardark, about 50 miles west of Toronto, in the year 1868, which as you will recall was the year following Confederation. In those years the Canadian oil industry was just getting established. There was a small oil field about two miles north of our town. Like many of the townsfolk, I had invested a dollar or two in this project. Alas the promoter of the field proved villainous. Our money was lost and the field was sold surreptitiously to a gentleman known only as "X". I was chosen to go to Chicago on behalf of the investors and confront X in his office. This was the longest train journey I had ever made and I arrived tired but happy to be in a larger city than I had ever seen before.

I located X with some difficulty. His office was in the upper part of a two-storey frame house far from the business section. The lower half was occupied by a cobbler's shop and an old widow who kept a cow. He greeted me warmly but with some surprise. But picture MY surprise on finding that X was none other than my uncle Jacob, who had fled Canada with Mackenzie in 1837 and had never been seen or heard of by our family again. He was now the living image of my grandfather as I remembered him and I had no reason to expect guile from the descendant of a man who had been the pattern for honesty in his days, or indeed from a member of a family as distinguished for candour as our own. He quickly persuaded me that this purchase of the oil field was part of a scheme that he had long been cherishing, namely, to re-establish himself in Canada from which he had been driven by the grave, though hardly inexcusable, errors of his youth. He asked me then, as a relative and friend, to go to Ottawa and approach on his behalf that eminent Irish-Canadian politician, Thomas D'Arcy McGee. In return he would assign his whole property in the oil field to me and I could reassign it, as I saw fit, among the previous shareholders.

Our next few days in Chicago were filled with entertainments. He treated me with all the affection appropriate to a long-lost nephew. In particular we met many members of the Irish-American revolutionary organization called the Fenians. They were his intimate friends, he informed me, and brought much legal business his way (for he was a lawyer) and he in his turn did them a service when he could by smoothing their relations with their powerful opponents in government and church.

I set out alone for Ottawa, with the instructions (which were very precise) that I was to meet a certain Ottawa tailor called Whelan, who knew McGee well, and he was to stop McGee on the street long enough for me to state my uncle's business. What was my horror when, at the very moment Whelan was introducing McGee to me, a very lovely young lady stepped out from behind some fencing and shot poor McGee dead. That Whelan (whom I believe to be as innocent of this horrible murder as I was) was hanged for this assassination is a part of history.

My fate was hardly less painful. It is not well known that these Parliament Buildings [EDITOR'S NOTE: He is speaking of the first Parliament Buildings, those destroyed by fire in February 1916] contain a deeply-buried corridor of dungeons. Confederation came about in a troubled period, when the threat of war from the United States and of insurrection or invasion by the Fenians agitated all men's minds. Preparations were made, therefore, for the imprisonment without trial, should need arise, of state prisoners and in the greatest secrecy. I believe that at the time of Confederation certain secret powers were conveyed to the new Canadian government by the Imperial government in London to permit perpetual political imprisonments such as mine. These dungeons are not uncomfortable. Though some yards below the level of the Ottawa River, they are not damp. That they have not been overused, I can well testify, for in my 47 years here, I have been, save on one occasion, the solitary prisoner. That exception was an old man (who died of grief shortly afterwards) who had impersonated Sir John A. Macdonald for some days on each of several occasions when Sir John was indisposed due to drunkenness. Having in this role stumbled upon state secrets and rashly signed some state papers of the utmost historic importance, it was thought best to dispose of him in this manner.

Understandably I have been lonely. My guards are affable but of few words. I have been well supplied with newspapers. I have even been able to keep abreast of events in my old town of Habardark. Habardark has had 15 barbers since my time. At present, with four barbers, it seems to me to be rather overstocked, but it is a growing town. Charlie McCrown has been a good mayor. With the establishment of the munitions factory the war has been good for Habardark. If I die here in this pit, I hope I will at least live to see (or rather, read of) the defeat of Kaiser Bill. Whether I want to see the sunlight again or not I do not know. It would seem very strange and perhaps be painful to me. In a sense I have been dead these 47 years. All letters that I write are rejected by the guards and I receive none. But I have written this simple account on the margins and on the blank pages of my Book of Common Prayer. Perhaps it will tell my story one day to the people outside.

J. FRIMS, *Our Parliament Buildings: a Documentary History (1930)*.

THE CANAL

All my grandfather's money went into building his canal. There was therefore not much money left for his daughters. Supercilious young men labelled them the Canal Sisters. Destined by their excellent family connections to marry into the highest families of the land, poverty dashed their hopes of matrimony. They sat at home year after year, playing the piano, painting watercolours, supervising the servants when there were servants or doing the cooking and cleaning whenever my grandfather's fortunes dipped even lower than usual.

No one bore this constrained way of life with less ease than my mother's favourite sister, the brilliant, fun-loving, red-haired Lucinda. It was a surprise to no one when Lucinda eloped with a red-haired Irish labourer at the canal. The marriage was respectably performed by Father Murphy at the works village (though we were Presbyterians) and when my grandfather learned that the young man had a good farm of his own in Western Ontario, he relented sufficiently to give the young couple his approval (grandfather's fortunes were very low indeed at this time) and even a few shares in the canal. It was a great novelty for us to have Irish relatives and although our relations were not of the warmest with them, the sisters wrote steadily and some visits were exchanged.

My grandfather's fortunes meanwhile continued to sink. The canal that was to make the fortunes of seven towns along its bank remained a half dug out trench of bed-rock and quicksand, much troubled by the landslides that poured into it every spring from the Mulbert Hills. Sir John A. Macdonald himself came to view the trench during the election of 1878 and out of pity for my grandfather, who was always a good Conservative, offered him a fine job in Ottawa if he would abandon this heartbreaking folly.

But my grandfather was not a man to exchange the rigours of commerce for the ease of a soft chair in Ottawa and besides, at this time, a new avenue of hope opened up. His young Irish son-in-law had come back to work for him one winter and proposed that the whole scheme be refinanced by a means he heard had come to be widely used in New York. Money could be borrowed for commercial enterprises in almost unlimited quantities and virtually without security. But the interest was very high, almost 100 per cent per annum, and if not paid, the investors took vengeance on their creditors, maiming or even killing them.

My grandfather was filled with the desperation of an old man who had seen his life's dreams frustrated for years and he cheerfully sent his son-in-law to New York to arrange the loan. The money poured in, work was resumed on the canal for about the fiftieth time – and by the end of the year the canal was open – to be wholly sealed the following April by a great mud slide which rolled down from the Mulbert Hills as smoothly as a freight train, filling it to the brim. The farmers said it reminded them of a pig trough filled with ground oats swill. My grandfather died of a brain seizure and my mother and the other unmarried sisters fled to Toronto, where they dispersed themselves under disguised names among the cheapest boarding houses. Their Irish brother-in-law, whose name was Donnelly, fled with his wife back to his farm near Lucan in Western Ontario.

Almost immediately afterwards the public of Canada was horrified to learn that intruders, supposed to be neighbours, had broken into the home of a family called Donnelly near Lucan and had murdered virtually the whole family. This massacre, one of the most celebrated events of Canadian history, was *NOT*, however, perpetrated at the expense of *our* Donnellys. Though undoubtedly intended by the New York usurers as a blow at my grandfather's son-in-law, they had attacked the wrong Donnelly family. A peculiar inscription, carved on a tree stump outside the Donnelly home and never explained by the police, was the emblem, well known to initiates, of the vengeance of these bloody-minded usurers.

What was our family to do? It was clear that they had escaped a most terrible danger. It was clear also that another, innocent, family had suffered a gruesome death in their place. It was also clear that the usurers were now convinced that they had taken the vengeance they believed necessary and were not likely to bother further with our family, unless they were stirred into action by being informed of their mistake.

Our kinsfolk took the course of wisdom. The Donnellys left Lucan, migrated to Montreal and, under an assumed French Canadian name, became one of the wealthiest families of that city. As I write, rumour whispers that one of them may become prime minister. My mother and her sisters became seamstresses and piano teachers in Toronto under assumed names, and in these plebeian occupations met and married a variety of respectable workingmen who found them, I trust, good wives. Perhaps years later they learned this strange story of their lives. It was noted, however, by the initiated, as a peculiarity in all these families that they always gave their children the names of the members of the murdered Donnelly family. It was as if they were trying, through a structure of names, to recreate a family to whose destruction they had been parties.

MRS. GEORGE OST, *A Canal and Its Secrets (1960).*

A TEMPERANCE FAMILY

Little does the hard-drinking teenager of today understand what a revolution the temperance movement was for his forefathers just a few short generations ago. For the young and aspiring, the temperance movement was the Apollo moon landing of the Victorian age.

Let us take my dear great-grandfather as an example. As a member of the drinking Haspern family, drink came to him as a birthright. His father, his brother and his uncles were seldom sober from the time they came home from shanty in April to the time when they shouldered their axes in October to return to shanty. The line on which the Haspern farm stood was called the Drunkard's Concession and my father was born at its highest point, Drunkard's Hill. You were not a man in that family unless you had suffered delirium tremens. Most of them had seen snakes before they were 16. You may guess that the family was not very prosperous and such was the power of their vice that this was disastrously true.

The turning point came one evening in late August 1874. Let us picture the scene at the Haspern farm. The Hasperns' hay was spoiling uncut in the fields. The cows had broken through the fences the men were never sober enough to repair and were raiding what remained of the kitchen garden. The fields where grain should have been ripening to gold in the August sun were high with the foulest weeds. The roofless barn, ravaged by a cyclone in May, would provide the animals and fodder no protection from the winter weather. Inside the house the six Haspern men were recumbent in various stages of alcoholic stupor.

But listen! A distant music is drawing nearer. It reaches the drowsy ears of the drunkards and awakens them. The sound becomes louder. It is the Clairseach Temperance Band marching along the muddy road. It stops at the Haspern gate and pours out melody after melody. It is irresistible, to my great-grandfather first of all, then to all the other Haspern men after him. They break down, they weep, they seek the simple instruction of the leader of the band, they all sign the Pledge in the dying light of that August day – and a new life for the Hasperns has begun.

I should not be writing this simple memoir on a warm and lovely February day on a delightful island off the Yucatan coast of Mexico if the Hasperns had not learned to make money after their sobering up. I guess our family has made a penny or two since then. My uncle Jacob was supposed to be the richest man in Calgary in his time. But that is a digression. Back to my great-grandfather.

To return to shanty for another winter was unthinkable. Shanties are places of sad temptation. He decided to try instead for commercial wealth. He sold 40 acres of the family farm, all that was his inheritance, and with the money enrolled himself in a course at MacMurchison's Business College in Ottawa. The following June he set himself up as a storekeeper at the little railway village which his enterprise was soon to make a bustling place and is now known as Haspern's Station. For the next 50 years he was the genial, well-known and well-loved merchant of a wide district. He was called Happy Jack. He was always smiling. Only one fault and one tragedy marred his life. He had a most explosive temper, and that was his fault. He was married and had six children but one day his wife disappeared. That was his tragedy. She was never heard of again, poor woman. It was supposed some tramps (of which there were too many in the neighbourhood) killed her and buried the body. Everyone could see that this distressed the husband and children horribly.

Within two weeks all the children had left home. The oldest was 22 years of age, the youngest only 11. It was their great grief that caused them to leave but it was a heartless act because it left their poor father all alone at home so soon after his bereavement. It also gave needless force (and for this I blame the children most severely) to a malicious rumour, circulated by drunkards who hated his temperance principles, that my great-grandfather had slain his wife with a piece of stove wood.

But although he had troubles, people said he remained as happy as before. He was always smiling. He left an estate of more than $250,000 and his children, though they did not all follow his temperance principles, had absorbed so much of his business acumen that they all put their money to good use. I should say that they all got a share of the money early, as soon as great-grandfather was committed to the mental hospital. So you see the adoption of temperance principles by my great-grandfather was the turning point for our family.

HISTORICAL SOURCES. "A New Family of Converts", *Temperance Reformer*, Sept., 1874; – "A Family of Disgraceful Inebriates Converted near Haspern's Ferry", *Total Abstainer*, Sept. 1874; – "The Statement of Mr. Haspern and His Sons on Their Allegiance to Strict Abstaining Principles", *Temperance Man's Clarion*, Christmas Issue, 1874; – *Globe* (Toronto) and *Haspern City Advocate*, obits. of James Haspern, 20 Oct. 1925; – Mrs. George Jones, *A Genealogy of the Family of Haspern, A.D. 600-1960* (1961); – private information.

MRS. GEORGE JONES, *A Country Merchant (1980).*

COLORADO

In our village, as in so many other Canadian communities of the 1870s, the constant migration of the young to the United States was a cause of grief. The degree of grief varied, of course, according to who was departing, and it was at its lowest when the Wardsen boys departed.

What householder in that village had not lost at least one pane of glass to their depredations? My poor brother lost every window in his house in a single storm of stones the night he stopped one of the boys from stealing a plug of chewing tobacco from his store. Gardens were trampled underfoot, villagers' cows were let loose to be worried by dogs, gates were smashed, wheels on buggies were dangerously loosened, dogs were poisoned, cats were smashed to pulp under the pounding of heavy home-made boots and small boys on their way to school were turned back again whipped with nettles or rolled head to foot in tar. Where the depredations of the Wardsen boys extended into the countryside there were cases – never heard in court – of hamstrung horses and cattle and of burning barns.

It was no wonder, therefore, that joy was felt when it was known that they were packing their bags for Colorado. It was not even much diminished when their allies and cousins, the Framleys, took up a door-to-door collection for the price of their tickets and – on a rather large scale – travelling expenses. Then they were gone. Barely had their absence been fully appreciated when the rumor went round – they were coming back

The Wardsen boys had not been long in Colorado but their visit seemed to be remarkably profitable. In fact, from this time onwards, they were one of the wealthiest families of the county. That they had obtained their money by some crime no one I think ever doubted. They made a few short trips to Montreal and Toronto after this and then came an announcement – they were opening a factory for the manufacture of cook stoves.

Such were the origins of the Wardsen industries in which so many Canadians work today and on which the prosperity of our town depends. It would be pleasant to tell this tale as one of reformed characters but I owe it to my readers to confess that, in their new role as capitalist manufacturers, the Wardsen brothers were more like devils than before. What was previously a melancholy tale of rural outrages, such as many small communities could tell, became and has remained ever since a tale of grinding employers, widows oppressed and underfed children worked half to death in dangerous conditions. Flash fires were an almost yearly occurrence and unsafe machinery was used resulting in untold number of accidents with no hospital fees or compensation ever paid. Low wages were paid, if at all, and there was a system of fines that no employee could help breaking half a dozen times in the week. The Wardsens owned nearly all the stores in town and expected their employees to buy from them or lose their jobs and they had a grip on the very homes of their employees by being their mortgage holders. That the consumption rate in this town is one of the highest in the province can be traced back to the Wardsens in half a dozen ways. And how many deaths from typhoid have we had in the years that they have run the town water supply as part of their mill system? And how many deaths from fires in their tenements where the poorer workers live or their boardinghouses where the single workers live?

Here in Colorado, where I am spending the winter with my daughter and where I may remain for the rest of my days (which the doctors tell me will not be long) my thoughts are much on what I have seen. For me at least, life has come full circle, for it was, presumably, in Colorado somewhere that the Wardsens found means to exchange their bad characters for worse and to make our sleepy village the near city it is today. Somewhere perhaps in these mountains, under a pile of tailings or at the bottom of a flooded mineshaft, lie a skeleton or two which, if they could tell their story, would fill in a chapter in the history of our town.

JONATHAN MAS, *An Old Man's Days (1917)*.

A STORY ABOUT ALEXANDER MACKENZIE

Just outside the village, on the site now occupied by the Princess Margaret High School, used to be the sinister Mud Pond. Scientists tell us that this pond, popularly believed to be bottomless, was in fact a muskeg lake similar to those in far northern Canada. Many were the tales told by the old people about this pond. It was still told in my boyhood how in 1873 Alexander Mackenzie, about to become the first Liberal Prime Minister of Canada, attempted to cross this pond in a buggy in a dry season and sank to his death. He was immediately replaced in politics (so the story went) by his identical twin brother who served out the term of his administration with competence but without the fire and glamour his more enterprising brother would have supplied. It is probable (assuming the story to be true) that if this accident had not happened, Sir John A. Macdonald's later years would have been spent in opposition rather than in office. After the artesian well was drilled for the water works in 1930, the Mud Pond gradually dried up and became a patch of sandy ground on which I used to gather wild strawberries.

DONALD GREEL, *Clairseach, Ontario (n.d.)*.

93

A HARD SCRAMBLE

My father was one of Toronto's most affluent lawyers. We had a fine brick, three-storey home in the best area of the city and seldom fewer than six servants – every comfort that backward city could then provide. Of the circumstances that ended father's career I shall never say anthing. According to Burke, even the wounds of a father are venerable. But from that day to this I have never had the pleasure of using my own Christian name or surname. On the night of 16 December 1861, mother and I fled through the streets of Toronto. We spent the first night (unknown to our hosts) in the warm stables of one of father's clients. Thereafter we sought the hospitality of friendly farmers. Our story at this stage was always that we were a poor widow and her daughter travelling to Kingston to be at the bedside of a dying grandmother. But since Kingston society was merely an extension of that of Toronto, we had no desire to get there. We therefore declined the offers of a kind farmer called Bourbon Laclame to lend us sufficient money to make our journey by sleigh. Our real aim was to take refuge in some isolated community and there seek what employment might be available to us.

Accordingly we were glad to learn near Belleville that a rural community not many miles back from the river was anxious to obtain a schoolma'm. I had been "delicately nurtured", as the phrase was in the novels of those days, and my education had been mainly in sketching, singing, playing the harp and piano, polite conversation and similar drawing room accomplishments. But I had also somehow (perhaps because I was very bright) managed to acquire a solid core of knowledge of arithmetic, history, Latin, geography and such subjects as might equip me to teach in a rural school.

Imagine me then on the first Monday of February 1862, standing at seven o'clock in the morning before a class of some 40 ruffians of both sexes, ranging from five to twenty years of age, the sturdy sons and daughters of the rough farmers of the neighbourhood. How I laboured that winter! And how I suffered the insults of the big boys and the no less unendurable sniggers and giggles of the little boys and girls. But my time was well spent. My students learned something, perhaps for the first time in their academic career, and I got to know their families sufficiently well to spot the sons of the most prosperous fathers. I found that these were five of the older boys in the class whose fathers stood out in the community for their relative wealth. Of these five I eliminated three on grounds of evident weakness of character. The two remaining being to my best judgment equal in family standing and personal promise, I directed my campaign against the one that I regarded as the more handsome of the two. The struggle was brief.

Before the end of August I was the wife of a substantial young farmer and my mother (who had been ailing ever since the rigours of her mid-winter flight from Toronto) and I were comfortably established with him in a neat new log cabin.

In the years that followed I proved an excellent business manager for my husband. To his farm I soon saw added another, and to that I saw added saw and grist mills, of whose accounts I was the tireless supervisor for over 15 years. When we began to go into lending on mortgages I was the indispensible account keeper. An ample inheritance from my husband's merchant uncle in New York (whose existence I had noted before our marriage and with whom I had taken care to begin a long and steady correspondence almost immediately afterwards) almost doubled our wealth.

When my husband died in 1885 I was therefore left a wealthy widow. Regrettably, I had no children. Only my mother, who was still alive but very old and frail, remained to me as a family connection. I saw no reason to leave the community where I had been so successful and happy and besides, I had my eye by this time on a well-to-do widower who was thought to be a rising man in Sir John A. Macdonald's party. We married, and mother, before she died, had the satisfaction of seeing me the wife of a cabinet minister. The time will surely come, when my husband will have his knighthood and I will be addressed as Lady. The prime ministership itself is perhaps not beyond his talents. I heard someone say the other day that there will be a scramble for it when Sir John A. (who is a dear) goes. My life has not been a genteel one, but in the hard scrambling of this pioneer continent I am proud that I had the courage to play my part.

ANON. in *Memoirs from A Treasure Chest*, B. ZOMBS, ed. (*1913*).

A LOST MOWAT

My grandmother was an old acquaintance of the Mowat family and served as a domestic for a few years in the elder Mowat's household. She had a most remarkable story to tell, which I believe has never sufficiently been considered by historians. She was firmly convinced that at the age of 10, young Oliver Mowat was kidnapped by Gypsies and never returned. According to one tale which reached the Mowat family, he was sold as a white slave to a Georgia plantation owner. A family named Carter in the southwest central part of the state were his supposed masters.

When the Gypsies who had seized young Mowat were apprehended in

Kingston a few years later and brought to trial, they could not supply the missing youth but schooled one of their own children to pretend to be young Mowat. The Mowats easily saw through the pretence but accepted the youth, since a considerable inheritance from a great-aunt of the Mowats in Scotland was dependent on the child's return. This wild child caused the Mowats much distress for several years and more than once ran away and had to be forcibly returned to his foster parents. But at length he settled down and, as we know from history, was for 24 years Premier of Ontario.

My grandmother always followed his fortunes with interest and from time to time picked up some evidence which corroborated the story I have just told. She was well acquainted with an aged seamstress in Oliver's house and this old crony of hers often told her, over tea in the Mowat kitchen, that the Premier sometimes slipped down the back stairs in the dead of night and rode away for a few hours with parties of dark-skinned men who were unmistakably Gypsies. The cook in the same household was under orders never to turn away a Gypsy who came seeking a meal but to offer the best that the household afforded, and afterwards to show the caller up to the Premier's study, if he was at home. A distinguished German philologist who dined at the Premier's house during his tour of Canada and the United States sought permission to converse with the cook in her native language, which was a very rare and intriguing and almost extinct dialect of County Mayo Gaelic. In his praise of the Premier, the German scholar let slip that he, Mowat, was a most wonderful man, but the greatest surprise of all was that he was so perfect a scholar in the Romany (Gypsy) tongue, which he, the philologist, had never succeeded equally in mastering in 20 years of study.

I know from my own delvings that the Toronto *Globe* complained on several occasions about the activities of Gypsies in pro-Mowat electioneering and that Mowat commissioned the Cornwall, Ontario, law firm of Ol, Ceol, & Craic to investigate the alleged mistreatment of Gypsies in Dundas County in 1882. So perhaps there was more to my good old grandmother's yarns than an old wives' tale.

T. CRAWFORD, *My Home Town (1929)*.

THE RM

... the palatial brick mansion (NW corner of Square) now occupied mainly by the Prince Consort Insurance Co. was the home of OLBRED SMITHERS, one of the intellectual fathers of English Canada. He was born at An Cheathru Rua, County Galway, Ireland, in 1812 and died in this house in 1891. Olbred was a bailiff in the employ of the Hurry family, Ireland, for a few years in his youth but emigrated to Canada in 1835 and thereafter practised as a journalist. At various times he edited the *Clairseach Herald*, the influential *Toronto Clarion*, and many other newspapers and magazines. In his editorials he preached the doctrine known to historians as the Rural Myth (abbreviation: RM). Originally his invention, it was taken up by a multitude of politicians and fellow journalists and was very popular in late 19th century and early 20th century Canada. In recent years it has been the subject of a number of scholarly studies in Canada and abroad. It is the first topic in Canadian intellectual history to be made the subject of important monographs by scholars in Germany and France.

Scholars are agreed that the RM may be defined as the belief, once dinned into the willing ears of our forefathers and especially into the ears of rural voters, that FIRST, the farmer's occupation is incomparably the noblest in the nation (Olbred said that farmers are "a million Hercules behind the plow"); SECONDLY, the poverty, squalor, mortgage-sharking and other miseries said to afflict Canadian farmers in Olbred's day were either a fiction or rendered insignificant by the intoxicating delights of rural life (Olbred: "A song in the heart is the richest possession a farmer has. Mortgages are paid off with the most useless possession a farmer has – money"); and THIRDLY, the lives of rich railway speculators, property millionaires, industrialists and even the humbler run of mortgage-brokers, lawyers and *rentiers* are grossly unsatisfying by comparison with those of farmers (Olbred again: "The secret of every rich man is that he wants to be a farmer. The truth about nearly every rich man is that he doesn't have enough character to go and do what he wants to do. I often envy the farmer. I never envy these poor weak rich men").

The purpose of the Rural Myth, back in the days when the farmers' vote was still important in federal and provincial elections, was to undermine the belief of farmers in the causes of their discontent. Between 1868 and 1870 Olbred preached his views with such force that he is reputed to have been almost single-handedly responsible for suppressing the nascent Poor Farmers' Party, which formed in the aftermath of Confederation and for a few years made such inroads into the support of Sir John A.'s Conservatives. In the financial panic of 1873 he persuaded farmers to quietly sell their farms to satisfy their creditors and seek healthy, invigorating jobs as hired men in the green meadows of their solvent neighbours. In the 1870s and '80s he was credited by the Toronto *Globe* with having done more than any other scoundrel alive to reconcile farmers to extortionate interest rates.

His economic theory that farmers who received incomes below the cost of production were in effect *"Raised to Solvency"* by their *"Invisible Income"* in the form of fresh air, happy, satisfying outdoor work and the multitude of pleasures provided by an isolated rural life was received respectfully by economists. The concepts of *"Raising"* and the *"I. Inc."*, which feature so strongly in the works of the late 19th-century agricultural economists, are directly drawn from his teachings. Through the writings of his most influential academic disciple, Elmer Skroop of the Department of Economics, University of Chicago, he is believed to have influenced the Chicago monetarists of the 1980s.

One of his projects was the reform of the Canadian Senate. The Senate, he believed, was a relic of the past and should be replaced by an assembly of typical farmers, nominated by the government. The farming population, having a whole branch of the legislature to represent it, could thereupon be disfranchised with respect to the parliamentary vote, thus relieving the farmer of a concern for politics which so often cut into his valuable working time and weakened his enjoyment of the pure and wholesome pleasures of rural life.

His views did not always find the admiring acceptance which, by his later and more intolerant years, he came to expect. In 1881, while crossing a lonely stretch of depopulated farming country north of Clairseach, he was hauled from his buggy by a band of husky young farmers and tarred and feathered. Goldwin Smith said that Olbred did not know the difference between a hen and a cow. Sir Wilfrid Laurier said that Olbred's admirers did not know the difference between Lazarus and Dives.

A frequent guest of the rich, Olbred developed a reputation as a connoisseur of wine and food. Under the guidance of experienced friends his ventures into the stock market and property investment were almost invariably happy. He owned shares, which were often gifts from well-placed friends, in every financially successful railway in Canada.

Olbred left an endowment in his will to provide a $1,000 prize annually for the best Canadian poem in praise of rural life. The prize was a major influence in the Canadian literary world till the endowment was swept away by the 1929 financial crash.

Olbred's portrait was painted by Homer Watson and shows a short fat man with heavily spotted complexion studying a bust of Plato and a sheaf of wheat.

The SMITHERS' HOUSE contains a small museum of his possessions and exhibits illustrating his career, including a good reproduction of the Homer Watson portrait. Enter by the blue door on the left of the Prince Consort Insurance Co. sign ...

Literary Guide to Toronto (1981).

THE BERTAL BAY COUNTY
MURDER CASE

In its early days our town had as one of its founders a Japanese pirate and today one of its natives and part-time residents is among the most brilliant atomic scientists of our time. But in touching these extremes Bertal is not very different from any other Ontario Village. The most astonishing aspects of human life can be found exemplified in each and every Ontario village. Bertal's strength, like that of each and every Ontario village, is in its most ordinary people.

With this preface, which the claims of modesty and fairness have compelled me to make, I wish to assert once more the claim of Bertal to be the county town of Bertal Bay County and to express my indignation at the villainy which deprived it of this status 60 years ago.

At that time the horizons of all Ontarians were much narrower than they are today. It was perhaps in an attempt to widen these horizons that most towns had one or more Literary and Debating Societies, which often doubled as temperance societies. In Bertal the L&DS took up the temperance cause at an early date and its debates, on such subjects as The Justice of Bismarck's War on France, and Whether India Would One Day Be a Dominion, were conducted with the utmost propriety. The members were the most manly and respectable young men of the vicinity. On an evening in January 1890, when the Society was about to debate the question of Whether Tennyson Was a Greater Poet Than Longfellow, some surprise was caused by the appearance in the hall of a well-built man, with the dress and dirtiness of a tramp, who expressed, in a voice evidently marked by liquor, his ability totally to refute anyone who dared to defend in the least degree the merits of either poet.

In that light-hearted period, jokes of all kinds were more welcome than they are now and the meeting quickly agreed to let the stranger have his say. Let me abbreviate the events of that evening by stating that never were opponents to a motion more devastatingly defeated in the Bertal L&DS than they were by that half-drunken old tramp that evening. As midnight approached, and midnight was a very late hour in those times, the unkempt debater stepped out the door without a word of warning and disappeared as mysteriously as he had come. All this would have been forgotten long before our time, had not the horribly battered and torn body of the tramp been found the following morning not 20 yards from the door of the Lord Dufferin Hall where the debate had taken place.

I think I can say with honesty that the criminal charges which followed were never proven or even given much credence. Five members of the

L&DS were brought to trial for the murder of the stranger. It was shown that they had used abusive language to him before he left the hall and had been seen leaving the hall, apparently in pursuit of him. They were all acquitted and the real murderer, his motives, and even the means by which he so hideously mutilated the body, have remained a mystery to this day.

But for Bertal, this was not the end. Its powerful enemies in Bay Town now mobilized their forces and by an appeal to an outraged public opinion in the county, quickly stripped Bertal of its ancient honour as a county seat and had it reassigned to their own town. This honour had been sought by Bay Town for many years and has been gloated over to this day.

Gentlemen, I have studied this mystery for years, seeking the means to get back for Bertal its rightful honour, and I think I can say now, without fear of contradiction, that I have discovered the true murderer and that there is no reason why Bertal's standing as county town should not be reinstated without delay. (NOTE FROM THE EDITOR OF THE BERTAL BAY COUNTY HISTORICAL SOCIETY. The preceding document was found among the papers of our president Dr. Seeley when he died in Florida last winter. It seems to have been written about 20 years ago. Dr. Seeley probably intended it as an introduction to a larger treatise of which he used to speak on the Bertal murder case. It is a harsh remark to make about one to whom our society was much indebted, but it is to be feared that Dr. Seeley's defeat when he ran in the provincial election, and in particular the lack of support from his own village of Bertal, soured him enough to make him abandon his intended treatise and limit his dental practice more and more in favour of part-time residence in Florida. Dr. Seeley was a close man and never communicated to any of his friends the exact lines of enquiry on which he was working, much less the conclusions he had reached. The Great Bertal Bay County murder case remains as much a mystery as ever.)

Notes from Bertal Bay, Vol. 66 (1971).

THE TOWER OF SKULLS

From our neighbourhood has spread one of the most horrific legends of rural Canada. What are the details? It is alleged that when the first pioneers came to this area they found, in the dense vegetation of the primeval forest, a tower of human skulls. The tower was conical and from a base about six feet across rose to a height of 20 feet. The pioneers broke the skulls in fragments and buried them in the Pinehalt sandhills. Many years later the wandering artist W. K. Moreton drew, from elderly men's descriptions, the sketch of this tower which is hung in the National Gallery in Ottawa and has been so often reproduced in popular history books. The date on which the tower was discovered was not preserved but it may be calculated from the known dates of settlement in this area to have been about 1820.

Such is the story the public believes, but what are the facts? I am sorry to say that I have grown convinced, after nearly half a century of studying this legend, that the truth is much, much worse than the legend, gruesome though the legend is. First of all let me say that the tower really existed, that it really was six feet wide at the base and 20 feet tall and that it really stood on the spot to which tradition assigns it, the little spur of rock at the corner of what is now the New Furniture Factory yard. So much can be established. But the date of finding it was not 1820 but closer to 1900 – long after this was a township of settled farms and prospering villages. The painting by Moreton was not made from old men's descriptions but from the very tower. I have been able to procure copies of more than 20 photographs of the tower. Photography, of course, did not even exist in rural Canada in 1820. In these photographs it is possible to identify a number of persons who were alive well into this century. One of them was my grandfather.

What was the story behind the tower? So impenetrable a silence has cut us off from the true history of events that we can only draw deductions from what scanty evidence exists. The lot on which the tower was *"found"* (we may now more accurately say *"built"*) by the local farmers was owned by the Rodge sisters. A family of hermits, they spoke to no one, seldom left their cabin and were content to let a new forest grow up, more impenetrable than the one their industrious parents killed themselves clearing from the land. Such a farm was an ideal place for the secure construction of an object of horror. But what was the source of the skulls? Now that a relatively late date for the tower may be established, the mind flies at once to another unsolved mystery of Canadian history. The Grand Route Londoner Express entered the Lambrook Swamp on 28 August 1899 carrying more than 700 passengers on their way to the Sons of Scotland Picnic at Ottawa. When the train was found that night, lying on its side by the track just beyond the exit from the swamp, it was empty. To this day the fate of the 700 passengers has remained a mystery. I calculate that 700 skulls would be just sufficient to construct the tower described.

It now remains to be determined how the conversion was made from 700 living passengers to a barbaric tower of 700 skulls. Obviously a considerable number of people must have been involved in the crime. But who were these criminals, and what were their motives? Here we must point the finger of blame in the first instance at a substantial farmer of the area, Nigel Jacobsen, who spent the first 20 years of his working life as a trader on the Upper Amazon. He was always an exotic figure among the humdrum, stay at home farmers of our area, but we may all too justly fear that the strength of personality which made them re-elect him again and again as reeve led them also into darker ways than have perhaps ever been followed elsewhere in Canada. My research shows that in the very area of Brazil where Jacobsen traded, the local religion, a form of witchcraft, was centred about cone-shaped towers of skulls built on stone outcroppings in isolated groves. A Brazilian government document (translated for me at the University of Waterloo) records Jacobsen's expulsion from Brazil in 1882 for *"promoting cannibalism and human sacrifices"*. An anthropologist from Brazil whom I have been privileged to consult has informed me that the *"cone"* religion, as it was called, is now extinct but that it gained its force from the consumption by the Indians of a powerful intoxicant, based on a local weed, which rendered the Indians insensible to all feelings of pity or horror while they massacred their victims and prepared their towers of horror. I have now found examples of this weed growing in the area of Jacobsen's old farm. They have been definitively identified for me by the Brazilian Department of Plant Research.

From these facts we may now report for the first time what happened on that hideous day of 28 August 1899. The more minute details, from which the mind recoils with loathing, we shall never know, but it is clear that in some way the train was derailed, the passengers seized and marched away by Jacobsen and his drug-maddened farmers and the massacre (no scene of bloodshed or violence was ever found) perpetrated somewhere in the depths of the swamp. The skulls were perhaps cleaned of their flesh by boiling and their transportation to the hermits' farm could easily be carried out in farm wagons. The bags in which they were carried must have had a helpful resemblance to bags of turnips. The tower was constructed under Jacobsen's supervision probably in the fall of the same year. We may acquit the hermits of any principal share in the guilt for what had taken place, though it is probable they knew what was going on.

Jacobsen died suddenly of a heart attack at a barn raising in the spring of the following year. With his death the satanic company lost its leader. Without him to share the guilt, an anguish they had not previously felt must have been experienced by his followers. The artist Moreton drew the tower about this time. I find from his correspondence in the National Archives that he had been a friend and sometimes guest of Jacobsen almost from the time of Jacobsen's return from Brazil. Quite likely he was in some way cognizant of the whole conspiracy. The tower was probably demolished in the fall of 1900, or at the very latest in the early spring of 1901. Almost immediately, to cover up what had happened, a spurious story was put about of the finding of just such a tower by the first settlers about 80 years before.

Since these grim events our community has remained as peaceful as any in rural Canada. One wonders, however, whether a sense of guilt, passed on and made hereditary even among those who had no knowledge of the terrible events between 1899 and 1901, has not eroded it like an acid. Our population is barely 40 per cent of what it was in 1901. A flight to the prairies and to the cities in the opening years of this century deprived most of the local families of their sons. Few of the substantial farmers of Jacobsen's day have representatives in the community today. Only a few houses remain in Medlar, Jacobsenville and Aster, our three most promising villages of 1900. It seems that Poulett Thomson, our most important centre, will never grow into a town. The tragedy has not been confined to our small communities. I often wonder why the artist Moreton committed suicide in 1905?

I am too old a man to have the vanity to want to publish anything but if my daughter thinks differently after my death, I urge that she seek a decent publisher and avoid the cheap little paperbacks that have mistold the story of the tower of skulls too often already.

CAMPBELL ORTLAN, *The Tower Mystery*,
HARRIET ORTLAN, ED. (*1981*).

A CANADIAN JUNGLE

Who remembers that a square mile of African jungle once existed within 10 miles of Windsor, Ontario? Or who knows that the Ontario banana belt first gained its reputation as one of Canada's most temperate climates as a result of this jungle? Pepys Havelock, said to be a descendant of the 17th-century diarist, made a fortune in the Congo River trade, which he afterwards invested in an estate and mansion in the Windsor peninsula and vast holdings in northern Ontario mining lands. Havelock's father, an English viscount of great eccentricity, had replaced the Elizabethan mansion on his Wiltshire estate with a new style of house, consisting of one vast line or corridor of single rooms extending in a straight line over five miles of English countryside. His son and heir, Pepys Havelock's brother, had gone his father one better by rebuilding the Elizabethan mansion, room for room, in the deepest galleries of the family coal mines in Durham.

Encouraged perhaps, by these examples the newcomer to Canada's shores spared no effort to plant every species of vegetation known in the Congo jungles on a selected plot on his property. To the surprise of all, except perhaps their proprietor, they took root and flourished and swiftly-growing African trees, taller than any trees native to this province, soon swayed in the Canadian breeze and rippled the curtains of flowering vines that trailed down to the jungle floor. It was conceived by a team of university researchers who investigated this Ontario jungle that the mouldering vegetation cast off by the plants produced sufficient heat by fermentation on the forest floor to provide a protective climate competent to secure the jungle against such unintimidating rigours as the winter usually offers in the Windsor area.

The end of the jungle was sudden. In 1911 there came into the neighbourhood an aged beachcomber from Singapore, said to be the model for one of the most celebrated characters in Joseph Conrad's novels. He settled down to an unwashed and unshaven existence in a little hut just beyond Havelock's property. For many months he spoke to no one and he was seldom seen outside his door by the neighbours. If Havelock noticed his existence he gave no sign. It seems, however, that Havelock had once been married to the old beachcomber's daughter and the old man had reason to believe that Havelock's unkindness to her (if a more unpleasant word were not applicable in this case) had led to her death in Simla in 1876. One night, after a long period of drought, when a high wind was blowing, the old beachcomber slipped a gun into his belt and made his way to Havelock's mansion.

In the ornate dining room with its fabled display of glistening silverware, a bargain was quickly struck. The old beachcomber allowed that he had no wish to shed blood, and least of all the blood of one that his daughter had loved well, if unwisely. But he had lost, he continued, the thing that was dearest to him in the world. His notion of vengeance was such, he explained, that he could not rest in this world or the next unless he took from Havelock either his life or the thing that he, Havelock, valued most in this world. Well knowing the desperation of the old man who had committed, it is said, a particularly repellent series of murders in Rangoon in his youth in defence of a sister's honour, Havelock snatched at the proferred bargain. The two men marched out into the night where the wind was blowing almost a gale. Without a further word, when they had reached the edge of the jungle Havelock set fire to the dry matted undergrowth. Within minutes the sky was alight for miles as the jungle roared in its lake of fire; by morning only gray piles of ash remained of the most singular plot of vegetation ever planted by the hand of man in North America.

Havelock immediately abandoned his mansion and went to live on his mining properties near Sudbury. The beachcomber was never seen again. Havelock henceforth never left the north except for biennial visits to Paris. His mansion near Windsor stood empty for many years till it was bought and occupied in the prohibition era by an American gangster who died there in a hail of bullets in 1933. The site of the jungle is now being developed as a retirement village for the middle-income elderly. Havelock died in 1928, leaving all his money to promote the study of forestry in Canada.

P. FREUND, *Just Outside Windsor (1970).*

A LAURIER ADVENTURE

It is a fact almost unknown to history that, for four days in the Reciprocity Election campaign of 1911, Prime Minister Laurier was kidnapped and held prisoner near Hamilton by a Conservative cabal who hoped to force him to switch the campaign to an appeal for Imperial Union Now. His captors included your grandfather Thomas and his cousins Ernest and Frederick. Sir Wilfrid's campaign managers and the police foiled the plot, however, by representing to the public through the press in each of these four days that Sir Wilfrid was out of sight touring the smallest towns and darkest backwoods concessions. They supported this pretence by a steady flow of the Prime Minister's utterances from places actually non-existent. This ingenious hoax so discouraged the kidnappers, who saw that it put time on the side of the police, that they released Sir Wilfrid in the earliest light of dawn in the little muddy village of New An Cheathru Rua. After a breakfast of bacon and eggs in the temperance hotel Laurier was rejoined by his campaign throng and began a day of just the sort of backwoods campaigning the newspapers had been reporting. It was perhaps owing to Sir Wilfrid's exceptional charm that your grandfather afterwards changed his politics and served with such distinction in two cabinets of Mackenzie King.

Hapsburg Centennial Volume (1981).

ART HEIDLER

Looking back from the vantage point of 1933 we can see the 50 years or so before the Great War as the golden age of the hired man in Ontario. In those days every farm kept a hired man or two. It is not often realized that among the perhaps tens of thousands of hired men who circulated from farm to farm in those days, were some who later achieved fame and fortune in endeavours far removed from pitching hay and shovelling manure. But who can say that they did not learn lessons during their stints as hired men so valuable that without them their later careers would have been impossible?

It is not absolutely proved, but it appears pretty certain, that in the winter of 1890-91 Rudyard Kipling worked for my great-uncle James as a hired hand. This young Englishman gave his name as John Smith (there were a lot of John Smiths among the hired men of those days) but the verses which he recited, and which my great-uncle and his neighbours learned by heart, were printed years later under Kipling's name. When the lending library finally got a picture of Kipling in a back issue of *Harper's*, there weren't many doubters among our neighbours that Kipling had been the hired man. Ralph Connor was preaching in our neighbourhood about that time and had many intimate conversations with our John Smith. It is questionable whether Kipling's influence inspired him to begin writing his series of romantic Canadian novels of adventure and heroism. I should add that my cousin Jack Burstin has read this and wonders whether it wasn't Ralph Connor who pepped up Kipling and got him ready for all the writing he did after that.

But perhaps the most intriguing connection of all came in 1911 when my brother George hired a sickly-looking but cheerful enough young German called Arthur Heidler to help him with his sheep farm. When we learned that the hired man was an artist and painted landscapes, we all laughed at George. But the young man proved a good worker and George said that for upkeep of barbed wire fences he had never seen a better man. He didn't get much chance to do his painting though. George didn't leave him much time on weekdays, when farmers and hired men alike worked from dawn till they went to bed, and the minister warned George that it was wrong for his manservant and a stranger within his gates to paint on Sundays. This Art had a poor stomach and ate like a bird. Sometimes, when he was asked, he would say Grace in German at the meals. He was not a good mixer but used to go to the dances at the Grange Hall and stand with the other tongue-tied boys at the back. He was a strong temperance man and when we would pass around the bottle outside the hall, as we always did, he would never take a drink. He began to show signs of wanting to keep company with old man Schlossfuth's daughter, but the old man said that whoever got his daughter would of necessity get his farm (which was one of the best in the neighbourhood) and that no vagabond would get that, and so broke off the budding romance.

His employment came to an end in 1912, when George sold his sheep farm and moved to Manitoba. Art worked for a farmer at Clairseach Station for a few weeks, then left for Halifax, being on his way, he said, to Liverpool where he had relatives. Afterwards I understood from my brother in Manitoba that he and Art exchanged letters. Art's letters arrived first from Liverpool, where he seemed unable to find employment, and then from Germany, where he refused to seek agricultural employment again and seemed to be falling on very hard times. I believe my brother (who had a very soft heart) and his wife sent him money more than once. My brother was killed in the war and when a letter from Art arrived after the war my brother's widow threw it and all Art's previous correspondence, which my brother had carefully saved, into the fire.

My neighbours and I and George's wife (who is now back east among us) have put together all we can recall about Art, and we have little doubt that he is indeed identical with the Adolf Hitler who became Chancellor of Germany last January and is now so much in the news. But the only tangible relics we have of him are the initials "A.H." which he carved on one of the beams of my barn during threshing time. George's wife says we hear so badly of him now, that she wonders whether it was he that robbed the bank at McClairseach in broad daylight about six months before he arrived in our neighbourhood. But one thing is sure, if he was living on old man Schlossfuth's farm today as one of the industrious farmers of this neighbourhood, his name would not be in the world press and hardly even in the press of Clairseach Station.

R. MACDONALD, *Clairseach Station: The First 75 Years (1933)*.

TWO BROTHERS

I was addicted from an early age to travel. My father's little farm, with its 70 acres of cedar swamps, where our cows were often lost, and its 30 acres of stony *"cleared land"*, had no attractions for me. I went to the California gold fields in my youth, to the Cariboo gold fields in the 1860s and, in the mounting pains of my rheumatism, I climbed the passes to the Klondike in '98. But it was in Alaska in 1903 that I knew I was old. I returned to my father's farm where I found that little had changed. My mother and father were dead and my brother, who owned the farm, had grown old like me. The swamp had proved as intractable for him as for my poor father and 30 acres of barren land could not support as many as half a dozen cows. I helped him for a few years with the chores. Like myself, he was an old bachelor. Then the urge to travel came on me again but this time I only went to Toronto. I live in this little room now. You may not believe me when I say I am reasonably happy. When I die they can bury me anywhere. When you have been a wanderer it does not much matter where you lie. Only I would not like to be taken to any of the medical schools.

Quoted in R. M'RAE, *Old Bloor Street (1914)*.

I don't know why my life has been so disappointing. It has been disappointing you know. I have never lived anywhere but on this farm. My brother was a bit of a bum but he had enterprise. You could see there was fire in him. He was always following the gold fields – California, Alaska, even Australia, though for some reason he did not like to talk about that. I heard once that he had killed a man in Australia; another time the story I heard was that he had stolen something from the miners and they tarred and feathered him. I could never stand up to my father. I was timid then and I am now. He made me stay on in this hole of a farm where nothing will grow. You know what I have wanted all my life? Good meals. But I couldn't afford them on my income – though I ate well enough as far as just keeping body and soul together were concerned. I wanted to marry and have a cook but it was impossible while my parents were alive. After they were dead everyone seemed to have moved away: there was no one I could marry. I am too old now to care about this or anything else. My brother came back here a few years ago and stayed with me. I didn't welcome him when he arrived and when he left, it wasn't because I asked him to. He was free to do what he pleased. I could see he was restless because there is no company around here so he went to Toronto which is big. I will give you his address before you leave. It is on Bloor Street. I don't care how soon I die. When I die, this farm belongs to Queen's University.

Quoted in *Chats with Old Timers,* by *"A Journalist" (1914).*

THE TWO WORLD WARS
AND THE DEPRESSION

IN SEASON

In England the seasons move gradually, each one slowly, slowly, with every minute change merging into the next, but in Canada the change of seasons is sudden, dramatic, explosive. I'm no poet, no man of letters, but my father was both. Perhaps he could have described the Canadian seasons in a way that corresponds to my feeling for them. Alas, he never saw them (so far as I know), just as I never saw him. My own memories of England are dimmed by my absence of more than 50 years. But this great war that is now raging makes me think every day about the great country that gave me birth. When it is over, if it is ever over, and I am not too old or ill, I will gather up what little savings I have and travel to England, to explore once more my native land before returning to Canada, the only country in which I feel at home, to die. When I am in England I shall study my own reactions with such acuteness as I am capable of – and for a reason that I will indicate before I finish these pages.

It is an honour to have an ancestry such as mine. Will you believe me when I tell you that my mother was an earl's daughter? I must add that I do not know which earl, any more than I know the name of my father.

It is not difficult to earn a living in this country, but it is hard to become rich. In my trade as bookkeeper, I have never lacked employers for long. From my modest but steady earnings I have filled the rooms of my little house with books – not just books I cared for (for the truth is, I never cared for reading) but all the books of all the English poets and men of letters, major and minor, whose life dates were such that they could possibly have been my father. I believe more than 600 authors are represented here. It is possible that my father was not in the ranks of the first 600 but the evidence I was given – it was very little – says that he was among the top score of writers in his day, so you see, I have given myself an ample margin. I have read many of these books and as for those I have not actually read, I have in a way, by skimming and note-taking, so familiarized myself with their contents that I may be said to know them pretty thoroughly.

See these walls. These genealogical charts show the earls of the English peerage for that period which *must* contain my grandfather. Not a detail in these charts but is imprinted indelibly in my memory but, as to which of the earls is my grandfather, I am without a clue.

I was a good bookkeeper. Unfortunately, where the finer feelings are concerned, I was always a bit of a duffer. This has mattered a great deal to me because, as I mull daily over the books in my library, I try to detect in my own feelings, my own temperament, something that matches the elevated feelings, the noble expression in my books. But I am like a man in a fog trying to compare two mountains that he faintly sees. I have never understood my books; I have only made a muddle of trying to understand myself.

I have also made myself a great expert on the features, the temperament and the hereditary traits of the English aristocracy – for the same purpose of finding telltale echoes of those in myself – and to the same frustrating effect.

Now that this war has turned my thoughts homeward to my native land I begin to think that perhaps the clue for which I am searching lies not in what my feelings are in this country, but what they would be if they were called forth in response to the scenes that my father's and my mother's noble kindred knew. I therefore await the end of this war with fear and trembling.

O. SMITH, *Unfinished Autobiography of the Late O. Smith of London,*
Ontario (1917).

ANACHRONISM

The strife that frequently accompanied elections when I was young would seem very strange to those accumstomed to the tolerant and easy-going elections of today. Then election pranks were often of a rough and ready kind. I remember that in the campaign of 1886 a group of Conservative roughs spent the night digging up the sewage and water systems of our Liberal town and connecting them so that the sewage ran back into the water taps. Senator Topless, who was a great man in our area, is said to have laughed like a maniac when he heard about it. I fancy that such pranks would not be viewed so leniently in these disease-conscious days.

Among the most vivid of my youthful memories is that of being taken by my parents in our express wagon to view the mound of glowing coals which was all that remained of the porticoed southern-style mansion of our county's member of Parliament the morning after he lost the election of 1891. Such were the rude customs of the time and such the power of an MP that had this unfortunate man won the election, the torch-bearing mob never would have dared to approach his house, much less commit it to the flames.

My father was a well-respected blacksmith in the town and although interested in public affairs he always made it a point to keep clear of these commotions. He said that elections should never be a cause for a breach of good neighbourliness.

I am afraid these peaceable and Christian sentiments were not shared by my elder brother. As he grew up he showed an aptitude for electioneering that the next generation of boys was to show for auto mechanics. My sister still has the gold watch he was given by an unknown hand for his assistance in seven critical constituencies in the 1896 election campaign. I believe it was always his practice to assist several candidates in each campaign, not necessarily all of the same party. For although his political feelings were of the strongest kind, they were not confined to the defence of a single party. Rather, he loved the excitement of electioneering and freely let its emotions flow over him regardless of party affiliations. But times change and I am afraid my brother underestimated these changes when he undertook, in the election campaign of 1921, to secure the election of Ferdinand Reloops, a convicted bank-thief and one of the last potash entrepreneurs in Ontario, as member of Parliament for our county.

The methods being used by Mussolini at this time to put himself in power as dictator of Italy were unrestrictedly applied in the peaceful rural neighbourhoods and sleepy towns and villages of our constituency. A tale of burnings, beatings and intimidation overflowed into the urban newspapers with the result that, although my brother's candidate won, he was afterwards disqualified and several of his supporters sent to the penitentiary.

My brother fled to Germany where he took up our father's trade of blacksmithing and remained till Hitler became Chancellor in 1933. When he returned to Canada he said that the age of the blacksmith was over in Germany. He was at this time a Communist, which I fear had more to do than shoeing horses with his flight from Germany. He died in 1944. When I look back on my brother's career I reflect that he was one of those people who deeply understand the immediate past but do not so well understand the present or the immediate future.

J. BUAIGH, *Village to Subdivision (1950)*.

THE CHICKENS AND THE COUNTY

My grandfather was a giant in agrobusiness before his time. In September 1929 he had more than 100,000 half-grown chickens on his farms near Penumbra Station. A few weeks later the New York Stock market crashed and with it prices for farm produce. My grandfather saw that it was pointless to raise his poultry to maturity. It only remained for him to cut his losses. With tears streaming down his cheeks, he opened the doors of all his hen houses and turned out into the rich autumn countryside of Portal County the chickens that a few days earlier had been designated to be the crisp, crackling roast fowl of the nation's Christmas dinners or the stolid egg layers of the winter and summer. His bold act transformed Portal for years to come. The chickens adapted readily to the wild and when spring came set to work redoubling their numbers. Foxes so fat as to be almost bloated were a daily sight for years. Chicken hawks barely able to fly for their weight hovered uneasily overhead. Throughout all the hardships of the Depression people had an abundance of free chicken meat and free eggs daily. Nobody needed to sleep without good feather pillows and mattresses to soothe his rest.

Grandfather was amused with what he had done and wrote some humorous articles about it for the farm press. Unfortunately these came to the attention of the government, which promptly sold the shooting rights in the county to an American syndicate for $5,000 and an undisclosed sum in political contributions. For weeks that autumn the county was thronged with bands of American hunters blasting away at the chickens. By first snowfall there was not a single wild chicken to be seen. That winter the starving foxes tore hideously at the sheep and the poorer people of the county began planning their migration to British Columbia which took place the following summer. Grandfather got nothing out of this miserable catastrophe but if he were alive today he would be glad to know that no fewer than three Canadian novels of the last few years immortalize his feat.

M. MEEM, *Feathers! (1978)*.

BASE YEAR 1941

The years of the Great Depression were black years indeed for the inhabitants of our county. How hard they were can be documented from scientific data. It is well known that in this part of the province the groundhogs increase in 12-year cycles. The increase is steady almost year by year till the peak year is reached then, in the very next year the groundhog population drops off to almost nothing. Thus 1900, 1912 and 1924 were all peak years for groundhogs and so, in the natural course of events, 1936, 1948, 1960 and so forth should also have been peak years everywhere in this area. But we find today that *two* cycles are operating in this area. The old cycle of 1936, 1948, 1960 and so forth still holds good for all the area *except* for our county, where a new cycle has begun following the pattern 1952, 1964 and 1976. The explanation for this discrepancy is simple and appalling.

It is well known that we were forced to eat groundhogs during the Depression. Even those who lived in the more prosperous homes of the county knew the taste of a groundhog pie or stew. As for myself I still

THE CHICKENS AND THE COUNTY

occasionally long to taste that astringent meat again. But to return to our subject. So completely was the county scoured clean of its groundhogs in the Depression to feed hungry humans that the old cycle was totally suppressed. A new cycle was begun, as soon as the pressure on the groundhogs was released, in the base year 1941. In that year prosperity returned to the county with the opening of the flax mill and the bomb factory. The groundhogs, able to breathe freely again, began to increase their numbers from near zero-point to maximum population by 1952. Centuries from now, unless other catastrophes intervene, this strange discrepancy may remain to puzzle scientists and to remind those who are able to inform themselves of the truth, of the terrifying power of the Great Depression.

R. BOBS, *Looking Backward (1978).*

THE HISTORY OF MY FARM

As I have researched it this farm was purchased by my grandfather in 1870 from a Mr. McCready who wanted to emigrate to Manitoba. Who Mr. McCready was or what became of him, or whether he even reached Manitoba, I do not know. For that matter I don't know much even about my grandfather, or even about my father, except that I didn't get along with either of them in my childhood. With my mother dead they had the job of bringing up me, the only surviving child of the family, and a right morose pair to do it they were too. I knew what blows were. What I didn't know was either decent treatment or decent food. All we ate was garbage. I ran away to the States when I was just 12 years old and began the most adventurous period of my life. Some of the tales from that period I want to include in a separate history. This is to be just a history of my farm, though I can see I am wandering from the main thread even of that, but I find I don't care.

There was only one event in the history of my farm that mattered much to me, and I can see it is drawing my narrative in whirlpool fashion about it. I fell into some pretty rough company in the States. I spent the years 1920 to 1926 in prison. While in prison I killed a man in a fight but the authorities didn't find out who did it. His brother knew though, and when I was released I fled back to Canada pretty quickly. I never used my real name after my first year in the States so I thought, "Who can trace me? They can't find me on the old farm." When I got back my father was dead but my grandfather was still alive. He was so old that he never bothered me but let me farm as I pleased. A few years later he died of pneumonia and I was on my own. I was a little lonesome but I had a good stock of cows, 12 or 14 most years, pigs and sheep and always kept good horses. I ran the farm so well that people said I was one of the best farmers in the neighbourhood. I began to think of marriage.

But one evening in April, just when I was hitching up the horses, after my supper of salt pork and fried potatoes, to go back to the fields for another hour of plowing before dark, I saw someone walking up the lane to my house. I recognized the walk before I saw the face but I waited till I saw the face to be sure. Yes, it was the brother of the man I had killed. Knowing what he was after, there wasn't much choice for me, was there? I knew what I had to do and I did it. I buried him six feet deep that night in the field next but one behind the barn, and when the land above him had been plowed, disced and harrowed, who could have told that there was a grave there? I soon lost track myself of where exactly in that field it was. No one will ever find it. Nor does the crime bother me much. There were earlier crimes that should have troubled me more if I was inclined to be troubled by such things.

I don't think that my neighbours suspected what had happened. The murder took place at an appropriate moment. The victim arrived by daylight, but if he left after a reasonable period of time for visiting or for business, it would have been by dark, wouldn't it, and people wouldn't have been able to see him? Still, I don't know how it was but the marriage I had planned didn't come off and now she is married to a fireman in the town. My next door neighbour grew less friendly than before, then he moved away and now the farm is rented. Such is the history of my farm. You see why it couldn't be made public in my lifetime, and you can see too why it is really just the history of one event for me.

T. KASTEN in *Memoirs from Alainn County*, J. ROSTER, ed. (*1940*).

A DIFFERENCE OF OUTLOOK

PRESS RELEASE
A NEW SEASON OF BROADCASTING

JOCK MORD SAYS: – Some of the personal histories of the Depression were sad but others were full of joy. From Dolcaster County we find the extremes of the first-named attitude in the memoirs, called *A Happy Life*, of Miss Alice Ekfrid.

"The leaves of another autumn are falling on the old homestead. The wind and the rain sweep them onto the veranda at night and in the morning, dazed from a night of dreams, I sweep them off again. There isn't much traffic on the Bromson-Cogtale Road anymore. A few horse rigs, a few cars. Yesterday I saw a man walking. I cry a lot when I am by myself. In the afternoon sometimes, I hitch up the horse and drive into Cogtale. That isn't much fun. Now that the Depression has closed the mill, everyone I knew when I worked at the cafe has moved away. If only my brother Teddy hadn't left all those bills in town before he went out west! I would be more welcome with the merchants. All I can be grateful for is that in a few years I will be dead or will have the farm paid for."

The joyous side of the Depression, JOCK MORD ADDS, is found in the memoirs, called *The Sunless Grove*, of Bernal Troops, who lived in the same community.

"Many were the joys of those golden days. I particularly remember the Hallowe'en of 1938, when 16 or 17 of us husky youths raided the barnyard of Jockiel Oorzt. He was never a well-liked man since he gave his prize bull to the Red Cross in the Great War. People said a man that good had something on his conscience. We had no trouble prying loose the boards at the bottom of his big wooden silo, the biggest in the county, and then cutting through the uprights with his bucksaw. After that it was an easy matter to turn the whole old silo over on its side in the farmyard. There was a clap like thunder when it hit the barnyard mud that was heard at MacDonald's Dance Hall six miles away. In the week that followed he had to stuff some of the spilled fodder into the cellar of his house to have a place for it for the winter. We had to laugh. That was the fall, too, that Jake Estir broke his leg trying to climb into the upper story of Fred Esbester's hen house. When he got back from the hospital, we didn't half give him a t and f. Lawyer DePort, who defended us, said it was the best tarring and feathering in the county in years. But it was a pity we had to do it to a man who was bedridden and whose wife and children, to his positive knowledge, never ate meat once in a month, and whose clothes, being rags, were not decent enough to be seen out of doors to go to school or to church. After that some foolish people even raised a fund for Jake and his family but our Teddy, who was a real card, got to be treasurer and absconded with the fund when he went out to Saskatchewan to get that legacy from his aunt the next spring. We had to laugh. Happy, joyous days of youth! I look back on them with ever increasing fondness as old age creeps upon me."

As the first of our *"Open Your Eyes to the Social Conflicts"* series of telecasts for this autumn, we are fortunate to be able to present "Confrontations from the Dirty Thirties" in which the authors of these extracts, Miss Alice Ekfrid (now Mrs. F. Burns) of Toronto, and Mr. Bernal Troops, a retired well-driller living in Hamilton, confront each other in the studio under the direction of our prize-winning interviewer, JOCK MORD,* who knows how to make the sparks of social controversy entertainingly fly. CKVN: The Tops in Educational Television, 8-9 pm, Tuesdays.

*MR. JOCK MORD is the author of *Mao, Our Guide to the Eighties* (1965) and *The Seventies, the Decade of Revolution* (1966) and many similar works. He is now writing a book on *How To Live Through the 1990s*.

YEATS IN WINTER

I wonder how many of the pretentious, highfaluting people who study Yeats in the universities know that he was here in Captainstone, Ontario in January 1933? Or that I have a book that he autographed for me and notes of the conversations that we had, day after day, for a whole week? All these are very precious to me and I will never sell the book or let any of these blathering baboons read my notes.

What attracted Yeats to Captainstone was my bachelor uncle Amadeus, known as Amadeus Angels, or the Captainstone Prophet. The reader who did not know Amadeus, or Yeats either, may smirk, but Amadeus claimed he saw angels day after day in his fields, his orchard, garden and in his house, angels gathered so thickly he could barely squeeze his way among them to do his farm work, make his meals, fetch his letters and newspaper from the mail box or keep firewood in the old wood-burning stove. A little pamphlet about Uncle Amadeus circulated in English occult circles and it was this pamphlet that caught Yeats's attention. Yeats, as is well known, was most deeply involved in the occult. I understood from Yeats that a few men like Uncle Amadeus were described in books written hundreds of years ago. It was advised that anyone who was a seeker after wisdom and who heard of the existence of such a man, should cross to the ends of the earth, if necessary, to sit at his feet in case he should be willing to divulge even so much as one unexplained and outwardly meaningless word of his wisdom. Yeats stayed at the Green Spruce Hotel, which I am afraid isn't a very clean place now and wasn't very clean then, but most of the local people invited him out for meals so he didn't have to eat anything at the Green Spruce but breakfast anyway.

Uncle made us free to call on him every evening but I understood Mr. Yeats never got from him any of the wisdom he was seeking. Uncle didn't talk much at best but all his talk at this time was about the crops, the weather and politics and asking what was London, England like? Yeats in return told us about London and about Ireland and the civil war they had just had there. He told us a lot about Patrick Pearse and Arthur Griffith and Michael Collins and the Men of 1916 and afterwards I read books and found out who they were. He had met Lloyd George recently and Lloyd George had heard about Uncle from that same pamphlet and hoped to meet him some day. One evening Yeats read us his latest poems, including some he said he would see were not published till 100 years after he died. He said that Captainstone was not ready for poetry yet but that it would have a great poet one day when we were all dead.

Mr. Yeats was a very modest man and I understood he was hurt because

Uncle, who was a great cattlebreeder and had the best Holstein herd in any of the five townships around, would never offer to show them to Mr. Yeats. I questioned Uncle about this and he said Mr. Yeats was good company but that he was "city folks" if anyone ever was, and that he never drew city folks into seeing what they had no interest in seeing. I told Mr. Yeats about this and he replied that among the simple folk in Connemara in Ireland, cows and the most refined modes of feeling and speech had always gone together, and that his friend Lady Gregory, about whom he had been telling us, was a good judge of cows herself.

I shall try to remember Mr. Yeats as I saw him at the railway station the night he left. It was one of those bitter Canadian winter nights and the loose snow, dry as dust, swirled around his legs and ankles like wreaths of cigarette smoke or, as he said himself, like spirits that could assume no body except in the shifting atoms of the snow but even so longed to speak. He seemed to be all scarf, and as he turned and waved from the train doorstep his long white scarf made him look like a genie out of a bottle or like a spirit of the snow.

His visit was soon forgotten in our neighbourhood. Only in the 1930s and '40s, when uncle was reeve most of the time, there were sometimes good-natured jokes about him at the elections, that he was friends with a poet. People would say, "Amadeus Angels, will you write poems yourself about being reeve so often?" But Uncle was so even-natured he never minded them but turned their jokes aside with more jokes.

I was a very young schoolmaster when I knew Mr. Yeats but I consider this the greatest experience of my life. Later, when I had to take courses at university so they would let me keep teaching, I took classes in Yeats and, as I listened to all kinds of guff, I used to chuckle at the thought that I was the only person in the room who had ever been a friend of Yeats.

R. GAN, *Captainstone (1980)*.

MISS STRINGE

Miss Mabel Stringe, who died in 1950, was the daughter of Colonel Stringe who owned the Karkmore Carriage Factory and built the mansion on Maple Street where his daughter grew up and spent her last years. Miss Stringe spent the 1920s and '30s in Paris, moving in artistic circles. She helped to finance James Joyce during the years of his work on *Finnegans Wake*. With greater financial acumen than some supporters of great artists, she kept section of *Finnegans Wake* as security for repayment of loans. Owing to a disagreement with Joyce, some seven or eight pages of *Finnegans Wake* were never returned to their author. They were in the possession of Miss Stringe when she returned to Canada at the beginning of the German attack on France in 1940. She often showed them to visitors at her Maple Street home. A few lines that my aunt Mary was allowed to copy ran, *"Water nilly Corrib obscooring the hoo hov difficulterence gulls and swans for schoolfoolows between Feargus O'Connor and Dan O'Connell merpoliticians of seachange."* It is said that Joyce scholars, studying their author in microscopic detail, have detected at several points in *Finnegans Wake* breaks at which material equal to about a manuscript page in length was omitted. The association of Miss Stringe of Karkmore with Joyce doubtless explains the appearance in *Finnegans Wake* of *"Karkmeer"*, *"Karkmoor"*, "Kharkimoor", *"Karkmooresss"* and *"Kharkimooress"*, words which Joyce scholars have hitherto struggled in vain to elucidate. (Surely the last two refer to Miss Stringe herself, who like all the Stringes was dark-complexioned?) All Miss Stringe's papers, including these Joycean scraps, were burned after her death. Her mansion, demolished nearly a year later, is now replaced by the Colonel Stringe Bilingual School. An eminent Joyce scholar is said to have wept openly in Harry Brown's drug store when he heard what had become of Miss Stringe's papers.

THE CENTENNIAL COMMITTEE, *Karkmore (1967)*.

A VISIT FROM HEMINGWAY

Who now remembers Alex Lefron, the first president of the Almondsville Literary Society? Yet for some 20 years he was a figure of national as well as local importance. Charles G. D. Roberts and Duncan Campbell Scott among many others admired his essays. When he died in 1940, decades after his fame had passed, the *Globe and Mail* still thought it worthwhile to give him an obituary. Mackenzie King sent a note of condolence to his brother and recalled how often Lefron's sayings had been quoted by Henry Albert Harper and the University of Toronto undergraduates of the '90s.

As a writer, Lefron was basically a collector of thoughts. After his day's work as a bookkeeper at his uncle's saw mill he read long into the night, noting down his thoughts as he went. These thoughts, elaborated (he would have said *"jewel-encrusted"*) in the most rococo manner of the belletrists of his day, he separated into their categories and sub-categories. When enough *"thoughts"* on one subject had accumulated to fill a paragraph he laid them side by side in logical order and, with a little further encrustation, welded them together so firmly that the paragraph did not break readily in reading.

121

Someone once said to me that the process was similar to that by which the Egyptians stuck their little strips of papyrus together to form a sheet. By a similar process of accretion Lefron's paragraphs grew into an essay and when he had enough essays to fill 80 or 100 pages he published another volume.

There were six of these volumes in print when the tranquillity of Lefron's existence was shattered in 1911 by the death of his uncle and his inheritance of the saw mill. Being now the wealthy proprietor of the sole industry of Almondsville his evenings were filled with the work of the mill. Seeing that the carefree evenings were gone, he appears to have realized that he had nothing further to lose by marriage and within the year was married to Marjorie, the daughter of the principal landowner of the area. Children followed but no more books.

It was at this stage that Lefron swelled into the figure that we knew in Almondsville for so many years. Obese, in every inch and in every pound the rich, small-town businessman, with his heavy, out-of-date Victorian suit, watch chain, walrus moustaches and too many gold and jewel rings, he drank and smoked heavily and was perpetually on the county council.

Not many visitors come to Almondsville except travelling salesmen and visiting relatives from the States. In the Depression there were even fewer, except for the tramps who poured through our town in profusion. But late one Wednesday afternoon in 1938, when I was just about to close my barbershop for the day, Donald from the hotel dropped by to say that a man dressed like an Englishman – Donald had been in England in the Great War – had checked into his hotel before seven that morning, ordered a bottle of whisky sent to his room and had been, as far as anyone could tell, asleep ever since. The next day news of the mysterious stranger – strangers, unless they were tramps, were all mysterious in our town – had spread everywhere. He was still, it appeared, sleeping and drinking. Another day passed and he continued to sleep and drink. He never left his room at all except to go down the hall to the bathroom. It was only late on Saturday, the fourth day after he arrived in town, that he called for a meal of bacon, eggs and toast to be sent to his room, dressed himself in a fresh white shirt and the tweed suit in which he had arrived and sallied forth from the hotel. He proceeded down the street to Lefron's door and pressed the bell. Twenty minutes later he was still in Lefron's house.

By now the town was all agog. From the number of lights in Lefron's house it appeared that some festivity was under way or perhaps just planned. But at 11:15, about four hours after his arrival, Lefron and his guest came out the front door. Lefron walked him to the railway station where he took the 12:05 train to Toronto, never again to be seen in Almondsville. Next day Lefron calmly confided to us that his guest had been the American novelist Ernest Hemingway. This novelist, he said, had become a great admirer of his essays and had called on him about a problem. About what problem he did not say nor did we ask. Most of us did not in fact know who Ernest Hemingway was but Miss Ermattinger, who worked at the egg grading station and was a mine of information on everything nobody else knew anything about, explained to us that he was a very great novelist.

Since then I have learned from a nephew of mine who studied literature at the University of Ottawa that when Ernest Hemingway worked for the Toronto *Star* he found Lefron's essays and became for a time so devoted to them that the other journalists nicknamed him *"Lefron"* Hemingway.

I have always been sorry that Lefron didn't invite us to get to know Hemingway in Almondsville. We would have asked him to contribute a recitation to a concert at the Orange Hall.

Clairseach Station was a lot more alert in its day than we were. You will all remember William Henry Drummond, who used to write the popular poems about French Canadians in the "habitant" dialect. When he was stranded by a train derailment at Clairseach Station the local people seized him and held him prisoner in their houses till he had written one of his habitant poems about the history of Clairseach Station. Of course they entertained him well all the time. He said when he left that he had never eaten so much fruitcake or pumpkin pie or such excellent preserves, and as to the baskets of food he carried away with him, well, as they say, it was nobody's business. All the same, he never did include the poem about Clairseach Station in any of his books, so perhaps he was more peeved than he seemed to be at the time. Lots of people around there still have copies of it.

Anyway to get back to Alex Lefron. When he died there was a surprise among his papers. He left six manuscript books of essays which he had painfully compiled over the years in his few moments of idleness. The style and the content were the same as before. He left them to the Almondsville Literary Society to decide whether to publish or to destroy.

Not being able to decide by ourselves we sent them to Hemingway for his advice. He never replied and the manuscripts were never recovered. Probably somewhere, somehow, they had got lost in the wartime disorder of the mails. But someone told us, perhaps as a joke, that they had fallen into the hands of a German officer in occupied France who spent his time as the commander of an occupied French town translating the six volumes into French.

PETER SOSS, *Almondsville (1959).*

A CHEESE FACTORY MYSTERY

When I was young, Fred Huneker was the richest man in our neighbourhood. The old folks used to say there weren't many pies he didn't have a finger in or many ways he hadn't thought of to squeeze the poor, but his main concern was a string of cheese factories.

This was the age when the cheese factory was going strong in Ontario. It's before the time of many of you, and even the buildings of these factories have vanished from the earth, but at one time the cheese factory was a pretty important institution in rural Ontario. They manufactured cheddar cheese, mainly for the British market. The first cheese factory began about 1860 and the last disappeared about 1950. And good riddance, I say! To get an idea of what the cheese factory system was like you must imagine something like a conveyor belt. At one end of the belt was a fat man in business dress, like Huneker, who owned a chunk of the system. At the other end of the belt was a crowd of farmers, as gaunt as concentration camp victims, who worked hard all their lives to supply milk for the insatiable factories and got only the meagrest living from it. It was an oppressive system, but in the countryside, in those days at least, people just buried their resentments and soldiered on just as if they didn't have any.

It was because of this way of thinking we had that our reeve Joseph Prender felt bold enough in 1944 to get up a testimonial to Huneker in honour of his 50 years in the cheese business. Prender was pretty much Huneker's creature, being married to his niece besides, it was said, being pretty heavily in debt to Huneker's son. To understand the story I am going to tell you, it must be remembered that it was the practice at this time for the kindly housewives all over the Ontario countryside to send "boxes" to the boys overseas. These would contain cookies, fruitcakes, maple syrup, warm socks and even some of Huneker's cheese.

Now as the evening for the presentation of the "purse", as people called it in those days, to Huneker approached, something surprising happened. Huneker couldn't be found. At first it was thought he had just gone to Montreal for one of his visits there. Though married, it was known that he kept a woman in Montreal on the side. But it soon began to be evident that he had disappeared in a more permanent sense and to this day, his family has never discovered what became of him. A blood patch on the floor of his buggy was the only clue ever found. There was a search high and low for the body but it was never discovered. Some people thought that he had fled to the United States. Some people thought that there was perhaps another mistress besides the one in Montreal who was being held by the police.

But my father told me a thing or two and now I will tell you. The packages that went out that fall to the boys in Europe were 50 per cent more numerous than before, and these extra parcels, all wrapped up in a special way, were sent out to the Hollis, Burling, Swetson and McCalla boys.

Huneker's cheese business was run afterwards by his son and his daughters now have what remains of the old Huneker fortune invested in Florida real estate.

I. J. IPSWICH, *True History of a Country Town (1981)*.

THE OLD HOMESTEAD

I was born in 1940 on a little rocky farm that my father had purchased on the glacial ridges north of the lake. I believe that the original owner of the land had simply abandoned it during the Depression. It later came into the hands of Mr. Jones, the Mayor of Callaghan, in payment of a debt at cards and it was he who sold it to my father for $2,000, a very large sum in those days.

My father could only make a small downpayment and how he had to squeeze his family to keep up the mortgage payments! We hardly ate any meat but bologna from one year's end to the next. Tinned beans were our only luxury. For long periods in the winter, bread and lard were our diet. In the winter, you see, when there was little work to be done on the farm, it was not necessary to keep up our strength. The farm itself did badly. The yield barely sufficed in good years to enable my father to keep up the mortgage payments. In bad years, which were common, it did not even do that. When my sister fell sick, we had her treated by a neighbouring squatter who knew *"doctoring"*. She died and I think my father was glad, for she had been one mouth extra to feed. From the age of about 10 to 14, I was almost never without a cold and a sore throat. I am sure my parents thought I would soon follow my sister. We all dreaded the winter. The drafts that whistled between the thin sawmill slabs that did for boards on our house made any kind of comfort impossible. There was never enough fuel. The house itself, which was of the crackerbox variety, was exposed to every wind on a high treeless hill. I left school at the age of 13 to help my father on the farm.

I consider that my turning point in life came at the age of 17, when I was crossing the highway to borrow some hay-loader slats from a neighbour and was struck down by a fast truck carrying horses to a racetrack. When they had amputated my leg I got a job as a government clerk in Toronto. Soon I was able to send some money to my mother and father to make their life easier. They now live in an old people's home near Wiarton. I am married and have two children, and I never drive through farming countryside without a shudder. I am grateful that my children never will need to know anything about farm life. I even hate the sight of the zoo and never take my children there. When people talk of the enjoyments of rural life I tell them politely as I can that they don't know anything about it.

OSBERT ROYALE in *Rural Days*, MILLICENT AND PRISCILLA DUN, ed.

(1978).

LOCAL HISTORIANS ARE ALWAYS A LITTLE TOO LATE

This remained a *"dry"* township till 1945, so we had bootleggers. Only one of this venerable crowd is still alive. That man is Freddy Verck. In preparing this book I interviewed him at the Op Hill Nursing Home. His memory was mostly gone, but he had flashes. On a good day he told me his story. He was a poor farmer, ruined by the Depression, who lacked food to put on the table for his children, so he turned to bootlegging. This would have been about 1936. Later good times returned but by then he had kidney trouble so he continued bootlegging till 1945. Once the township was "wet" his trade was gone. He had a hard time till he was able to go on pension about 10 years ago. He was a lifelong total abstainer himself, as his mother taught him. That way he didn't get blinded on the bad whisky that circulated about the time of the Allied invasion of Sicily. Only one of his customers got caught on the whisky and he was sorry for him. *"He's dead now anyway,"* Freddy said glumly.

When I left Freddy Verck's bed in the nursing home I asked the nurse on reception if his son, the doctor, ever came to see him. She said no, and that he was too sozzled to recognize the old man anyway most of the time.

I would not have seen Freddy Verck again if a totally new and unexpected piece of information had not come into my hands a few weeks later. We local historians love to circulate information among us and a real blockbuster reached me from a friend whose niece is researching Canadian government security in the Second World War. It seems that a double agent who was under surveillance by The RCMP had stopped at a red-headed country bootlegger's home in 1943 in one of his ramblings. There he purchased a bottle of whisky which destroyed his sight and nearly killed him. He lay ill for weeks in a Montreal hotel room. Before he recovered, he confessed that he had left some of his secret papers, containing the names of certain suspect government officials, at the bootlegger's home. The *RCMP*, having seen the papers before they were planted on him, had no wish to see them again but retraced his steps to locate the bootlegger and mounted a watch on his home to see who might come in search of the papers. After the double agent had checked himself out of the hotel, he was never seen alive again. A badly decomposed body, thought perhaps to be his, was found floating in Lake Ontario a few months later.

Remembering what Freddy Verck had said about the poisonous whisky, and that his hair, like that of the bootlegger the secret agent encountered, had been red at that time, I decided to interview Freddy again.

I found the old man lucid but in tears. Word had reached him just hours before that his son had died in a car accident, a victim of his own drunken driving. In Freddy's condition it was impossible for him to consider attending the funeral. In view of this misfortune, I naturally set aside all thoughts of broaching the question about the secret agent on this day but Freddy, who was now quite alone in the world, so strenuously implored me to stay, that I settled down for the afternoon. Since other possible topics of conversation were lacking I soon advanced the question about the secret agent. Had the secret agent visited him and, if so, what had become of the papers he had left behind?

To my great surprise the old man claimed that his house had been a recognized "safe house" for secret agents. Some dozens of conspirators came there every year during the war to exchange messages and he particularly remembered the agent he had inadvertently poisoned and who had left behind a briefcase full of papers. Normally, his house being a recognized safe house, the police would have arrived within a few days or hours to retrieve the lost objects. But this time nothing of the sort happened. The briefcase remained in his keeping till the end of the war, when he burned it and all its contents. Had he examined the contents before burning them? Yes. His experience had taught him that it was not wise for him to know more than he needed to know about these matters but curiosity got the better of him. I could see his mind was growing dim now with the sedative that the nurse had given him but he added, when he could pull himself together a bit more, he could piece together a part of what he had read. The results, he added, might surprise me. Had I heard of a man called Albert Speer?

That was the last time I ever spoke with Freddy. His mind became so clouded immediately after this that I could never be sure he recognized me again. The nurses report that he never speaks an intelligible word to them.

Now I read in the newspapers that his son was suspected of being a Communist agent and was the veteran of many trips to Cuba and Rumania. What tale of intrigue slipped so elusively by me in our quiet township at just the last stage at which it could have been disentangled?

P. POPL, *Pioneers to Us (1975)*.

JAIL BIRDS

In the southern part of your county the Adirondacks of New York State are seen as a range of blue mountains. From the northern part of the county the highlands across the Ottawa River are another chain of blue mountains. But you were born and lived all your life in the middle of the county, where neither of these mountain ranges can be seen. This is a neighbourhood of cedar swamps and low-lying farms. Where the ground happens to be high and dry, as sometimes happens, it is thick with rocks.

Your great-great-grandfather settled here and in time his farm came down to you. You never farmed it though. That is to say, except for two years about the time that Laurier came in as Prime Minister. Instead, you were a hired man pretty much all your life. It could even be said that you hardly lived at all. A hired man lives in other people's houses, does other people's work, eats in other people's kitchens, is cared for by other people's womenfolk – and is looked down on by everyone.

Your life seems to have had only a single turning point. That came one rainy spring evening in 1880 when your stepmother threw you out of the house. Your father was away at the time drinking, and one of your half-brothers teased you for a long time beyond what you could endure. You struck back and your stepmother acted at once like a trap snapping on a muskrat. I can see now that she had planned for this moment for a long time and knew exactly what to do. You wandered through the yellow light that fills the spring landscape when the sun breaks through the rain clouds just at the horizon. The cedars in the swamps glowed yellow and green in the bright new coat they get in the spring. The McAlpins, who lived not very far down the road, took you in and you were with them to the day I write this – 20 January 1945 – first with Alpin McAlpin, then with his son Colin and at last with Colin's young son called Young Alpin or Alpin Colin. You were never paid and you never expected it, for the McAlpins had no money, but you were as well fed, housed, clothed and supplied with pocket money as any of them.

But the strange thing to you was how your life sped past – 65 years since you left home and, except for a handful of those years, one was exactly like another. You stayed a virgin all your life. Only once when you visited Montreal with the other boys in your youth had you a chance to be otherwise and you were too shy to take advantage of it. You always worked desperately hard and you made your mark on nature that way, but nature, or the world, or call it what you will, did not respond by making an imprint on you. You feared it would make only one mark on you – when you died.

You saw two generations of McAlpins grow old and saw young Alpin change almost overnight from a teenager to a young man with the first signs of an old man – signs you never acquired. People told you you looked barely half your age, which was 80 at the last, and you never felt old. You never felt, in fact, any older than you were the evening your stepmother threw you out. You died, an old man with your life still to unfold, like a clock that stopped the moment its spring began to unwind. Life never had the same rules for you that it had for anyone else. But did you ever let those rules that were made for you operate in your life?

At this point let me clear up for the reader (if this note will ever have a reader) the questions of identity. The hired man was my half-brother Robert, and Robert died this morning. I am a prisoner in Kingston Penitentiary and in view of my long sentence and the circumstances of my crime I am likely to remain here till the end of my days. Robert's letters have been my eyes to the outside world for more than 30 years. Reading over what I have written (and I thought I was writing of what he had written to me) I see that I have written the history of my own life and that our lives were as alike as two peas in a pod.

B. McRICKT, in G. SMITH, ed. *Kingston and Its Prisoners (1950).*

AN HONEST MAN

What is an honest man? Well, I will tell you your uncle Ronnie was one. He didn't get to be mayor of Glampton without being an honest man. We were brought up to be honest at home. My father believed in whipping. His constant saying was never a boy or a girl but was bettered by whipping. They made him stop teaching his school on account of that but it was his motto and he stuck to it, at home and abroad. Otherwise we would all have grown up to be Big Demons. We were little terrors to begin with.

Your uncle Ronnie got married as soon as he left high school. Your grandfather didn't like it but said it was for the best. Ronnie went into the export trade. Everybody says the export trade is a nice clean trade. It certainly was for Ronnie. He exported Canadian goods to the United States. This was in the 1920s and '30s. Afterwards some change of regulations in the American government put him out of business. This was about 1933. But you cannot hold an honest man down for long. Everyone always said Ronnie was like a ball. He bounced back, and the project to develop the county farm as an industrial centre gained his attention for the next few years. He got to know a great many people in politics. I have seen

MPs, MLAs, and Senators arrive at his home. The county farm was not a success as an industrial centre but the government let the investors sell the land to meet their expenses. Ronnie used to say that if it was not for that county farm he would be rich. Still, I have heard it said that he did well out of it. He was very modest, or as though some people said very close. I have often thought that if he had a fault it was this closeness. It is not good to be close, even with your relatives. I have often questioned Ronnie about that business of the farm but he remained close.

Then the war came and Ronnie went into the merchandising line. His store was small but he did a great business. People came from as far away as 20 miles to buy from his store. This was never true of the other merchants in the town. In 1944 he became mayor. Many people were jealous of him at this time. They said he was in the black market. They said he sold nothing but sugar and tires. Even after the election these charges continued. There is nothing like politics to stir up jealousy. People even said the reason he was elected was because he knew something about everyone in town. An honest man has to put up with a lot of libel. He is a puzzle to other people so they lie about him to make him more understandable to their tiny minds.

Ronnie remained mayor till 1950 but you could see at the end that his heart was not in it. He was longing for change. But why did he want so much change? The change he had set his heart on was too big. One day we all learned that he had suddenly left the country, gone to live in California. His wife remained here. She was nice but I always found her dull. You could not take to her the way you took to Ronnie. Perhaps your uncle himself will write you something one day about his life in California. In that hope I will close this memoir of him here. It is not often that you find an honest man.

MRS. F. HASPWELL, *A Genealogy (1952).*

A LIFE REVIEWED

Yes, I am happy to give you an interview. What? Busy? No, how could I be busy at my age ? Only don't bump my legs when you bustle about. With arthritis, every touch is torture. Remember that. It will be something for your old age, if the world lets you get that far.

Yes, I was born on a farm. Everyone was born on a farm those days. Regretted leaving it? Never in your life. I leave that kind of nostalgia to city folk. Farm life is always *"blue remembered hills"* to them, isn't it? I remember the mud and the manure, the smell of the cows and horses, the flies, the milking at dawn, mother, who was always ill, father, who was always cross as a bear, Aunt Nettie, whose brother fleeced her of her little savings and dumped her on us, where she worked like a coolie, unpaid of course, poor thing – what other delights would you like to hear about? The cheese factory, which put the poor farmers on the rack and made them work for peanuts till they died? Then their sons strapped themselves in and boldly told the racksman to give the machine another turn, that some fresh young muscle wanted to try its strength. Or about the school system, where Miss Minue, who had hysterical crying fits during the lessons, was a perfect type of the virginal model turned out by the Normal Schools in her day? She was as ignorant of the world of books 40 years after she began teaching as on the first day she walked from her boarding house at Gustavesson's, where they had lice, to the little white schoolhouse, where nobody had removed the obscenities that the vandals had written on the blackboard with paint.

My older brother got shot up in the First World War and was never much good again. My father put him to work at jobs like picking stones, picking mustard, splitting wood, digging ditches, stooking and hay-pitching and sometimes, on days he was well, hired him out to the neighbours for such work as he could manage. But he got funnier and funnier in the head, as well as being crippled, and at last Dad had him sent to Brockville. Brockville? Yes, the mental hospital, the loony-bin. He died there in 1945.

I was about grown up myself when they put Fred on the train for Brockville and I had seen through farming. Yes, I took an axe to my father and held it over his head till he agreed to what I wanted – sell the home farm and give me the cash. He could live on the little farm we inherited from Uncle Willie, who died of the disease he got from all the whores he went through in Minneapolis. With the money I bought the feed mill and, as I learned how to make money, the foundry and the shoe factory. I worked hard and I was hard. Though factories were my business, I took care to keep a part of my money in farm mortgages. In my eyes, a mortgage was always the most profitable thing a farm ever grew, though for the farmer it was more like one of those vampires we see on television, wasn't it? I had a pretty good flock of these vampires tethered and feeding well for a number of years on the farms in my old township.

Like me ? People respected me. They knew what life was like. Don't tell me the farmers didn't know they were being swindled by everybody. They wanted to be swindled. Really did. People want to be defrauded, injured, raped – don't you know? You can hear about it today on those lectures on psychology on TV, but I knew it long before any of those doctoring fellows. The secret of my success? I had a lot of balls and other people didn't. Simple, wasn't it? The Depression? I weathered it. When I was being squeezed, I squeezed someone else a little harder. You can always squeeze a farmer a little more. People speak of widows and orphans but give me a farmer anytime for squeezing: farmers will work, but widows and orphans won't, so there is always something, even if it is pitifully little, that you can get out of a farmer. The war? I "did" the black market of course. A great business in those days, and a secret, unwritten, almost forgotten part of our history. I often think I would like to write about it one day, perhaps a book. I know so much. I was careful not to get too deeply involved of course. People got shot. Business friends of mine in Montreal lost their sons. They were shot for trying to cheat their suppliers or getting to know too much.

After the War I went into real estate. What I acquired then increases in value now every day. But since about 1960 my interest in life has been travel. I am only in Centrustown about half the year. I want to see every country on the globe. When I have to travel in a wheelchair, I travel in a wheelchair. Yes, it's easier than you think. I am in pain, but I am happy. When I think of the circumstances I grew up in they make me sick, but I am glad I had vision and got out.

INTERVIEW WITH JEFF DeMAHON IN J. BOBS,
Centrustown's Hundred Years (1975).

A FARM TRAGEDY

MR. J'S STORY

My father kept us boys working hard. In every season of the year there was a string of exceptionally nasty jobs to be done. In the spring alone, we ditched and picked stones, we plowed, disced, harrowed, seeded and rolled the land.

When John got the T.B. and had to go to the sanatorium, the rest of us had to work harder. Father himself was drinking a lot at the time and was an ugly customer to deal with. At first John made all the meals, because his weakness made him slow for field work, but after he was sent away we all took turns. I shall hate salt pork, salt herring, baked beans, potatoes boiled in their jackets and blackstrap molasses till the day I die. I always told my wife never to let me see them on the table.

When John died father was so far gone in the drink that he might as well have been dead too. Milt and I wanted to put him in the nuthouse in Brockville but the doctor said we had no grounds, and perhaps he was right. We worked out a solution anyway. Father went to live with his brother, another widower, west of Brantford, and Milt and I were left to run the farm, subject to sending father half the profits annually. There weren't any profits any year after this. Though the old man and a lawyer threatened, you can't get blood out of a stone, which is the saying, isn't it?

By this time Milt and I were not pulling together very well. When the war began shortly afterwards, Milt joined up. He served six years and was wounded. He settled in Cornwall after the war and worked in the paper mill. After father's death I had to let him sell half the farm as his share, though I should have got it all as the eldest. I haven't see Milt in 20 years and I don't want to see him. He is married and has two children. Both of them are in college and even his wife has a college degree.

I married too, though rather late in life. I was past 40. I was working part time on the roads for the council at this time. There wasn't enough money in farming, not for the amount of work you had to put into it. Everybody on the road gang was always talking sex. That set me thinking there was something missing in me not being married. Then after the companionship of the day, I felt lonely during the evenings. Television didn't help. One of my buddies on the road gang had a widowed sister. So I took her out a few times and proposed to her and she accepted me.

The marriage was not a success. She went back to her sister a few times, then finally she went back and stayed. The last I heard was she was in New Jersey. I also hear she has cancer. I got to hear after the wedding that she had had a lot of men in Cornwall during the few years she was a widow. I guess she had one after another. This was before she met me but I could never shake it off.

Perhaps I brought it up to her a little too often. I am back by myself on the farm again. I send milk to the creamery and manage to pick a living. My life seems to have passed quickly and I can't say it has passed unpleasantly. Sometimes I feel it should have been more interesting but I suppose television has spoiled me.

MRS. J'S STORY

My brother was like a father to me. I needed that, for my father and mother were weak, weak, weak, just as I have always felt myself to be weak. My father was sometimes a tailor, sometimes a drover, now and then a handyman, worked at one time or another but never for long as a salesman in nearly every store in town and sold liniments from door to door. My mother busied herself with her housework which, after the way of drudges, she never finished. Her house was always dirty and, for all my faults, I have never been able to stand dirt. If it hadn't been for my brother, who everyone said was as brisk a lad as they had seen, we would have been the most despised family in the whole town.

When I was 16 I got a job as waitress in the White Horse Cafe. They say old married men in small towns will not try these things but the owner was always after me. It wasn't that I was a good looker, I wasn't. But I managed to save myself till I married Bob Rice, who ran the shoestore. The war was on but Bob didn't have to go. He had a collapsed lung. After that we ran the shoestore together and that was the happiest period of my life. Our first child was born, then a second, both my dears died within one week from

133

whooping cough. I fell sick with pleurisy for a long time after that. It was odd that when I was well again, it was just as if the children had never been born. I occasionally find myself wondering whether I merely imagined them.

The proprietor of the shoestore wanted it for his son about this time, so we were put out. Bob and I moved to Cornwall. He couldn't seem to settle down in any clerking job and his health didn't permit him to do outdoor work. In the end his uncle got him a job answering the phone for the truck company he worked for. But Bob didn't do well there. He was sick a lot of the time and his work suffered. I find office work doesn't agree with people with weak lungs. In the end they gave Bob a sum of money and asked him to leave and I got a job cleaning for rich ladies, who were really just the wives of ordinary businessmen. Bob got another job, as assistant to a bricklayer this time, but it was his last. He had a cancer in his one lung by this time and was dead by the end of 1960. The bricklayer paid him the last six weeks of his wages, even though he wasn't able to work.

After this I lost interest in Cornwall and went to Montreal for a while. I worked as a cleaner in an old folk's home there. But I found Montreal too French so I came back to Ontario. I wouldn't go back to cleaning. My back was getting bad. I got a job instead as a waitress in a cafe. By this time my brother had a good business in Cornwall but it failed soon after. He was never afraid of hard work – and I can say the same of Bob, hard though his life was – and got a job for himself almost immediately with the county. He worked on the road gang and that was how I met my second husband. The men sometimes came for coffee to the cafe and my brother introduced me to one of his workmates, a bachelor fellow about my own age. Everyone urged me to try a second marriage with him so when he proposed I accepted and became a farmer's wife.

Being a farmer's wife isn't much fun. My new husband wasn't abusive, but he was a sneerer. Everything he said was sarcastic. I made lots of mistakes but I could have learned. But he kept at me with his jeers and that took the heart out of me. He was one of those men who can't do it in bed, if you know what I mean. We did it once before we were married but never after. Instead of trying to be a good husband he went around to the beverage rooms asking everyone what they knew about me and was told a lot of lies. Then he told them to me – horrible, unbelievable charges. I couldn't take his abuse and walked into town to my brother's place. I looked after a sister who was poorly and now sister and I are both in the States, looking after the children for her daughter. I had a non-malignant tumour removed in an operation last year and am now recovering nicely. For all that has happened, I was sorry when I heard of my husband's death last month. It must have been a terrible way to go. There will be a legacy for me. Mrs. Lucas has asked me to write this memoir to go with a sketch my late husband wrote and following her directions, I have done the best I can.

Two Memoirs from Honeybrook Farm, MRS. L. LUCAS-DOYLE, ed. *(n.d.)*

THE MODERN AGE

A TOUR OF THE TOWN

... In this house lived a retired sociology professor, Jim Milson, who taught the sociology of education for 25 years in Toronto and other large cities. His years of retirement were spent in the study of old spelling books used in the province of Ontario. He was fascinated by the many references to servants in these books. For instance, a child in 1920 might be given this sentence for spelling practice, "The maid is cooking the eggs in the skillet." By such a sentence, some students were prepared for the good life in which they could afford to keep servants. Others were prepared by it for a life in which they *were* servants. Jim collected more than 50,000 file cards and a nephew promised to process them on a university computer to sort out the social implications of these references. But Jim died before this could be done and his relatives, who were discontented with his will, shredded the cards. I should know because I am his brother and I flung the cards into the shredder myself. In a way, what happened was a pity because some sociologists think this study would have revolutionized our ideas about how the Canadian class system was crystallized and would have supplied a missing link that brought the radicals of the '60s to grief when they tried to construct a model of the Canadian society.

Further down the street, where the red geraniums grow in front of the white gingerbread veranda every summer, one of the seven or eight murders our town has known since its foundation took place. In 1945 a soldier came home from the war and battered his father to death with a pump handle. The army had made a man out of him and he did the only thing a man would do with a father like that. It was bad enough that the old man was a terror to housewives who went downtown to shop and to his daughter-in-law and sister-in-law, who to tell the truth were not fussy where they bestowed their favours. It was worse that he hung around both the boys' and girls' playground and around Pipe Major Oliverson's sheep till the major had to start padlocking the ewes' pen at night. I was a pallbearer at his funeral. I know his son well; he runs the Senior Citizens' Centre, which is the big red building you see down at the end of the street. It's a great place to go for a game of billiards. I spend a lot of time there myself. He has a lot of stories about his five years in the penitentiary, especially about what the men do to each other when they don't have any women around.

As we walk to the Centre, we pass Fred's Cafe. It is closed; I had to foreclose the mortgage myself. Fred was no payer and neither is Mrs. Smith, who lives in the big white house with the cupola. She will not live there much longer if my son can get her ejected. Agnes Jones in the blue bungalow with the red roof has the largest collection of royal commemorative mugs in Canada and was imprisoned for three weeks in Boston last summer as an IRA arms supplier. People used to think she was *"on the game"*, but now we know that the men who come to her house late at night are terrorists. Having them around is one of the inconveniences of living so close to the border. I handle all her legal affairs. She is said to be a descendant of Daniel O'Connell, the famous Irish *"Liberator"*. The large brick house like a warehouse was built by a retired farmer in the 1920s. He made his wife and five old-maid daughters run it as a boarding house. It was high school students they kept mainly, in the days when high school students boarded in town. I can see the old women now on Monday nights hauling pails of hot and cold water up the stairs for the students' baths. He was my grandfather and I was his heir. I owe everything I am to him, and of course to the poor women he worked like teams of horses. Before we turn over the tape, let's drop in at the Senior Citizens' Centre for a welcome cup of coffee.

From P. MILSON, Q.C., *"A Cassette Tour of Middleharvest"*, available from the author.

THE PHANTOM PAINTER AND THE MISSING PARADISE

LADIES & GENTLEMEN, Underman district shares in a mystery which I have long struggled to solve. For many years in the 1950s and '60s, during a few weeks about September when every roadside and neglected field was ablaze with goldenrod, an old white-haired gentleman, whose name we were never able to discover, used to appear with easel and oil paints and sit every day, in all weathers, painting landscapes featuring goldenrod. He lived and ate all his meals during his time with us at the King George Hotel being often the only room guest in that decayed hostelry and profitable drinking den, now swept away, to no honest man or woman's regret, by the tornado of last spring. A snapshot used this year on the cover of the Underman Highland Games Society's brochure shows the stranger leaving the main door of the public library about 1956.

By diligent inquiry I have uncovered the facts that a man of very similar appearance has been seen at work in two other parts of the province.

In Glengarry County he appeared every year in January and February to paint the drifting snow. Glengarry, though cold and snowy, is, it is well known, drenched in brilliant sunshine through the late months of the winter to a degree that is hard to conceive by those of us who live in the misty, smoky southwestern corner of the province. Nowhere else in the province, it is said, does the drifing snow, as fine and dry as desert dust, provide such a spectacle of colour as it clutches in whirls and eddies at the sunbeams like kittens clawing playfully at the ends of curtains. I have heard it said that until a painter has seen the atmospherics of the Isle of Skye and the effects of drifting snow in Glengarry he has not seen colour.

In Waterloo County the same man (it is almost certainly the same man) came annually in March and April, and in painting concentrated on two problems: the almost indescribable red of the buds of the trees in that county as they swell towards spring, and especially this incomparable red as it is seen from the east towards sunset; and secondly, the delicate plumes of steam and smoke as they drift up through the branches of the trees from the innumerable sugar camps of that sugar-making county. It was noted by the *Kitchener-Waterloo Record* that he first came to Waterloo on 31 March 1951 and left by train for the last time on 5 May 1968. But even that admirably exact and complete journal never succeeded in learning his name.

It is much to be desired that someone would reveal what part of the province this mysterious stranger painted in during the summer. In a sense, a part of historians' knowledge of this province will be tantalizingly incomplete till we have that knowledge. (Yes, Underman has the best goldenrod any traveller in this province has ever seen! The mineral content of the soil has been proved by University of Guelph tests to be especially congenial to it.) It cannot be doubted, then, that location of our painter's summer habitat will pinpoint something incomparable in the province, but which we will perhaps not know is such till he has pointed it out to our dull eyes.

But what of the quality of the paintings? Unfortunately no critic of the highest gifts has had an opportunity to view them. But amateurs of good taste and with good opportunities for comparison have been pleasantly surprised. In his private life our painter was as elusive as Turner, but I hope that before I end my pilgrimage we – someone – will uncover his lair, speak aloud his name and bring before the public a storehouse of paintings that may be one of the richest treasures of Canadian art.

"*President's Address*", in *Underman History,* 1981 volume.

THE PHANTOM PAINTER AND THE VANISHING PARADISE

IN TROUBLE

The Redmondville Historical Society doesn't meet very often any more. Its turning point came when Mabel Ostrax began pushing the idea that the basement of the Society quarters should be used for storing historic tombstones. These were being damaged at a pretty steady rate, you see, by vandals rampaging through the local cemeteries, so the idea got support enough to carry it. When the basement was about half full of these stones our landlord asked us to move so that his son could set up his dental office there. Getting those tombstones back up the stairs and into their new resting place in the back room of the BP garage was no small job I can tell you. It didn't help that Mabel Ostrax left her husband Fred at this time so he refused to help. As for those louts of Ostrax boys, nothing but an invitation to theft and vandalism could get them off the street corners. It is well known who broke all the windows in the separate school – though butter wouldn't melt in Mabel or Fred Ostrax's mouths. Then the bolt from the blue! – Martin Miller began a lawsuit against his brother Marvin for illegal disposal of the assets arising out of the dissolution of the Miller Brothers partnership. With our two leading members not talking to each other, even those of us who still clung to the Society didn't care much to urge the calling of meetings again. The last time we met there were just four of us – Mabel, myself, and that young couple from Clairseach Station who have been trying for two years to get credit at my store – which they will do, over my dead body.

The Redmondville Historical Society hopes for better days and until they arrive those among us who valued the society and the work it did will strive to keep the society going in name at least.

R. WIS, *"Note on the History of the Redmondville Historical Society"*
(privately circulated).

THE MILL MADE THE TOWN

The mill made this town, and now that the mill has been turned into a candle-and-pottery, arts-and-crafts factory, the town is coming to an end. The founder of the town was Ebenezer Craight. His keen eye discerned that the river that ran through the swamp in this place could be dammed to produce a good mill pond. He built his grist and carding mill at the outlet of his pond and for two generations it served the farm folk of this community six days a week. Around the mill Ebenezer laid down streets and built houses and soon he had a good town on his hands. It was low-lying but it was good. Out of that mill and his rented properties, Ebenezer's son financed three general elections and won all of them. He was a wonderful member of Parliament. I can see him in his frock coat and top hat now, just the way he looked when he attended his brother's trial. The next Craight was a poet but very business minded; he opened the Ossian subdivision when this town was really booming in the 1920s. He left three shy daughters but they all married far away and the mill was left to managers, not all of whom were honest with the Craights or had their hearts in the business.

When the mill closed for good in 1939 we thought the town would survive but we were wrong. Almost yearly since then there have been fewer people living here. When the window sash factory burned down it was not rebuilt. The foundry business dwindled till it could hardly be seen and now it too is gone. The newspaper closed just after the war. Geologists tell us it is owing to some shift of the land that the swamp is coming back. Our cellars are full of water. The Orange Hall has capsized because of the soft ground on which it was built. Even the mosquitoes are worse and people seem to have more colds. Property values have sunk because of the wetness. I see no future for this town. I fear there will only be a swamp here again in a hundred years' time.

MRS. CRAIGHT M'ONGLE, *The Town the Craights Built (1965)*.

A POLITICAL TRAGEDY

Diary of J. James, Reppton, 28 Oct. 1870: Neighbours horrified to hear of sad death of father. A fir tree falling on him while he was cutting caught fire from a spark from his pipe and poor father was a blackened curl of bones when we carried him home sorrowing. We have laid these sad remains on a clean white sheet on his bed for the wake.

Reppton Gazette, 1 Dec. 1888: We note with regret the death on the 20th ult. of J. James, 12th Conc. of Reppton. The deceased, a very respectable farmer of that area, had been ailing for a time till a pleurisy provoked by the cold weather of the past few weeks carried him off. It is this family of Jameses that has the curious legend that every second head of the family dies by fire, and that those intervening heads who escape the fire die by cold

... The first victim of the curse is said to have been a member of the family who was trading in India in the 18th century. He aroused a powerful witch by selling patent medicines to her customers and by way of retaliation she put this curse on him with prediction that it would last till a member of his family was both a Fat Wizard and a Great Governor in a Far Land.

Reppton Reporter-Gazette, 1 Oct. 1941: It is no exaggeration to say that the whole community of Reppton is in mourning today ... the sad death of the young airman, Carlon James, whose fighter plane crashed and burned ... a dogged fight against skilled enemies ... the Norfolk coast of England.

Toronto Gash, 1 Sept. 1962: A curious story surrounds the engagingly rotund young MLA whose marriage to the monied Miss Juxwood takes place today. According to an old family tradition, he is destined to meet his death by freezing ... His father, in accordance with the same prophecy, which is said never to have failed in 200 years, was burned to death. It is thought by some observers that a young man so well qualified and so well connected will not be allowed to freeze for long on the Conservative back benches.

Diary of Amanda James, Reppton, 27 July 1968: Returned from the funeral today of dear James. The politicians know how to put on a show at a funeral. Several people who know said to me that dear James was seriously headed for the premiership therefore I suppose it is just as well that his wife, dear Amanda, is burning all those trunks of occult books. What a strange hobby in a cabinet minister. He had one of those books in his pocket when the body was dug out of the glacier.

T. JAMES, *Genealogy (1972)*.

THE POND

My father was one of the best farmers I ever knew. Nothing was too much for him. From the day he arrived from Scotland to the day he died in 1948 he was always working and planning. He had 12 children. Michael, the next in age to me, was drowned in a pond we had at the back of the place. He was about 12 years old. The farm was only half-cleared and half-drained at that time, at least by my father's rigorous way of looking at things. Over the next generation or so his drastic reforms changed it out of all appearance. Among other things, he cut channels to drain the water from the pond where Michael died. Thus it became dry land. I plowed the shallow hollow more than 40 times in the years that followed. But I never did so without feeling that I was ripping up the grave of a brother I loved very much.

So when a legacy came to me 11 years ago from my brother, the engineer, I used that money to dig out that hollow again and flood it. I had the workmen follow, as nearly as I could remember, the old contours of the pond. I have planted some cattails and replaced a large stone by the water's edge in approximately the position I remember it. So the old pond is now much the way it was when Michael died. I often sit beside it on Sunday afternoons and on evenings when I have finished my work and wish that I was an educated man and could better express the thoughts that come to me. But these thoughts all too often seem to be from whatever I have been reading or seeing on television, so perhaps not much is being lost. In the drought two summers ago the pond dried up completely. I was sorry to see that but we have seldom had such a drought, and I trust it may be many years before anything of the sort happens again.

I. CLARKSON, *My Farm (1975)*.

INTOLERANCE

Local historians operate in a narrow sphere but with emotions that are stretched to touch the highest and the lowest levels of human existence. It is perhaps a combination of too narrow objects and too rich a burden of emotions that sometimes makes them shockingly intolerant to each other. I myself have known a local historian who wrote a pamphlet called *What a County!* to which his brother, who knew and loved the history of the county as well as himself but was desirous to degrade it because his brother praised it, replied with his own pamphlet, *What? A County?*

In the case of my own home town I am afraid that these passions have become so inflamed that when my history of the town appeared, the entire town council, followed by most of the town, as befitted a place where interest in local history rises high and passions run deep, poured out an indescribable flood of venom upon my book. But I was totally unprepared for the next step. The council, supported by a referendum, changed the name of the town and of every street and building I had mentioned in the book. The councillors persuaded their friends, the owners of the local factories, to change their company names, too, and used their influence with higher authorities to such effect that in the next few years they also secured a change in the name of the two rivers which meet in the town and

143

of the county and township in which our town is located. With almost every point of identification between my book and the town destroyed, I am afraid my book has little significance anymore except as a literary curiosity.

R. NEETZ, *A Leaflet in Reply (1960)*.